Father Eddie's Greatest Game

and Other Stories

by

Thomas P. Dwyer, O.S.A.

Cover: Bro. Jack Stagliano, OSA
Sketches: Mark Dwyer

Table of Contents

Preface

My motivations for writing this book of short stories about catholic priests are very mixed. I started writing in Japan as therapy to the stress I found in my life and ministry. I wrote many stories with Japanese and American characters. When my missionary life in Japan of fifty two years was finished due to illness, I returned to America and wrote my memoirs. I went through my files and found that I had some stories about priests which I thought were rather interesting. I wrote some more stories and decided to make them into a book. I had the stories edited by one of my Augustinian friends who is an expert in the English language. When I retyped the stories with his corrections and advice, I found that from a literary standpoint, they were a notch above my amateur writing. So my first motive was simply a reaction to stress. I had no agenda.

My second motive was my deep love for the priesthood that I had even in the early stages of my life. I had a wonderful missionary life as a priest among the Japanese people whom I came to respect and love. It was a big disappointment to me when I had to return to America. Even though my daily life was among non-Christian Japanese, I was always a priest and I felt respected. My priestly life was a pleasure. It was equally enjoyable to write about priests and the priesthood.

When I started rewriting my stories, a desire arose that these fictional accounts might become a shot in the arm for priests in the trenches or might plant a seed of a vocation in some young men. There are no models for my characters. It's all pure fiction and completely from my imagination. I guess my characters are composites of all the priests I knew since my childhood. There are comical, dramatic and heart warning stories that portray the spiritual and human dimensions of priests. I avoided controversy or any criticism of Church policy. I was impressed and edified by the many native and foreign priests I met in Japan. I found the Japanese Bishops to be fine men of integrity and good will. I am indebted to Bishop Dominic Ryoji Miyahara for the understanding, patience and advice in my last years. He is a man of deep faith.

I would like to salute all the Bishops, priests and deacons around the world. May you find peace and happiness in your works of ministry. Zeal for souls urges us on! There is an expression that is often used among priests: OREMUS PRO

INVICEM (let us pray for each other). Let us remain loyal to our Bishops and/or to our Superiors in the Religious Life. Let us be kind to our fellow priests and gentle in our words and relationships. I hope my stories will give you a chuckle and respect for all priests in the trenches or who have retired from ministry. Our fellow Catholics often ask us priests to pray for them. We beg our Catholic friends to pray for US too. With all our eccentricities and foibles have patience with us and pray that we will be good, loyal and zealous priests. St. Charles Borromeo, St. John Vianney, pray for us and through your intercession may our seminaries be filled with young men who are willing to give up their lives for Christ and His Kingdom.

Foreword

There are times when we, the people of God, need to remember to be grateful for the blessings that God gives to us. Sometimes we just take these things for granted and think that God just wanted to do it and it really wasted a gift. One of these is the great gifts of the priesthood and sometimes we do not ever realize what a great gift it is.

The priesthood of the Church happens only through the call of God through a vocation. That is, one who is attentive and listens to God, asking Him to respond to an invitation to serve the people of God in all their needs. These are not the people who aspire to be Bishops or leaders of the Church but those who want to satisfy the needs of the people for forgiveness and reconciliation with God and other human beings in whatever must be the struggles of life.

There are eleven stories in this book that tell the vocations of people who ordinarily in the Church are clergy. They listened to God asking them to serve the people of God in their needs. They were not seeking power in the Church. They wanted to serve the people in the realities of life. That means they wanted to be there to help when a child was sick or there was a death in the family or, there was for some other reason, a need for advice to help the family get along together by tolerance and forgiveness.

These stories of the clergy reveal them with their ordinary human eccentricities and each one shows that these peccadilloes at times created problems for themselves. But, the humanity they show in their service to others, makes them endearing always to the people. It is important for us to recall that even though they are members of the clergy, they are also human just like us. Like us they need forgiveness and, like us, they have peculiarities that make them unusual. But when we need their help, they are always nearby to be there to serve.

Some, like St. Augustine, are great saints. Augustine was acclaimed by the people to be ordained and immediately became their pastor and later Bishop until his death on November 3, 430. From his legacy came the Augustinians, who strive to find God in all the struggles and joys of life and to teach others to trust in God for eternal life.

3

Life at times seems to be a puzzle and we wonder about its purpose. Following Augustine, and supported by faith, we can see the purpose of life in both the struggles and pleasures but mostly in the love that God sends to us in family and friends. God tells us that the purpose of life is simple: to "love one another as I have loved you." In one of his greatest teachings, St. Augustine repeats the words of Jesus and tells us that we become one in our love for one another. The wisdom of St. Augustine tells us that God brings us together in friendship. The necessity of friendship among priests is reiterated in their superb books by Cardinal Timothy Dolan of New York and Msgr. Stephen Rosseti, Director of a facility for troubled priests. St. Augustine says: "The comfort I have in other friends and the pleasure I had with them in things of the earth did much to repair and remake me. All kinds of things rejoiced my soul in their company, to talk and laugh and to each other kindnesses, read pleasant books together, pass from the lightest jesting to talk of the deepest things back again; differ without rancor, as a man might differ with himself, and when most rarely dissension arose from our normal agreement, all the sweeter for it; teach each other to learn from each other; be impatient for the return of the absent and welcome them with joy on their homecoming; these and other such like things. Proceeding from our hearts we gave affection and received it back, and shown by face, by voice, by the eyes, and a thousand other pleasing ways, kindled a flame which fused our souls and of many made us one. This is what men value in friends."

Confessions of St. Augustine; Book Four; Chapter Thirteen
Fr. Neil McGettigan, O.S.A.
Villanova University

Dedicated

to

Francis Our Pope and Charles Our Bishop and all the Clergy.

Neil J. McGettigan, O.S.A.
Augustinian Friar and Editor of this book.

My Family
I love you so much.

Jim Murray and Arnold Macciocca
Thank you for your good humor, your understanding and your gracious support.

Father Eddie's Greatest Game

A few years ago when Fr. Edward Lewis directed the choir at the Papal Mass in Baltimore, there was an old gray haired priest seated among the clergy. It was Fr. Jimmy Garrity, who had taught the director when he was in the seminary studying for the priesthood. Who would have thought that that skinny young Polish kid would one day direct the polyphony Mass before the Holy Father himself, Jimmy reminisced with amusement. He recalled the legendary soft ball game between the "new guys" and the "world" (the upper class men) in the early fifty's. At that time when Eddie entered the seminary, it was a long and ancient tradition that, at the beginning of the academic year, the new students and the upper class men played a "getting to know you event" with a game of softball. The "world" had seven classes to choose from and always fielded a fine team. The "new guys", made up of only one class, had to field a team from their own limited members. In living memory, the first year students had never won. In sympathy for them, Fr. Timothy "Pop" O'Brien, the seminary spiritual director and an ardent athlete, always played first base for the new guys.

Fr. O'Brien was openly partial to athletes. He not only approved sports, he positively promoted them. He loved nothing more than to have a pickup game with the students who were good athletes. Sports, you see, were part of the seminary culture in those days. Those who were good athletes were called "pros" and those who were not athletically inclined were called "slobs." To Pop O'Brien sports were a good method to teach his charges team work.

Fr. O'Brien, who was a good left-handed hitter, often put the ball in the "pond" (the lake on the seminary grounds that was adjacent to the field) and would boast without shame, "Did you see that shot? I got some good wood on it." Some of the students who were good mimics would imitate him and say, "Did you see that shot? I put it in the middle of the pond."

A year before, when Eddie had an interview with Fr. O'Brien and another priest, Eddie was asked if he liked sports. To that question Eddie answered very honestly, "Not so much. I like to play the piano. My Grand Pop cries when I play Chopin on the piano. Do you like Chopin, Father?" This question made Fr. O'Brien very uneasy and he answered evasively, "Chopin? Yeah, sure, Chopin, yeah sure." Then Fr. O'Brien took a deep breath and asked, "you DO like some sports, don't you kid?" "Well, you know," answered Eddie, "I never liked sports very much. I like to walk in the woods and commune with nature. If you have a flower garden, I'll take care of it for you. What flowers do you like, Father?" Eddie Lewis was suspect.

Later, Fr. O'Brien mentioned to Fr. Garrity, the professor of mathematics, that there was this Polish kid who played Chopin on the piano and offered to take care of the flower garden. Fr. Garrity who was not much of an athlete himself, answered sharply, "So what? We will need a talented musician to play the organ and direct the choir. Johnny Ferry is getting ordained next year. This kid can take his place. The Polish kid will work out okay and probably become a good priest." "Well, I don't know. Those guys who like to work on flowers and walk in the woods to commune with nature give me the creeps," said Pop. "You're nuts," said Jimmy and walked out.

Eddie's ethnic background on both sides was Polish. Eddie's Grand Pop had an accordion that he had brought from the old country. They sang Polish songs and danced when they had a gathering. His Father had been a tackle on the high school football team. Even though he had a chance for a scholarship, he went to work to help the family financially. His mother was a kindergarten teacher who had talent for music which she passed on to the three children. Eddie loved the piano and practiced every day. Since Eddie showed an aptitude for music, his Mother hired a teacher to help him improve. His older sister, Kay, was already an accomplished cellist. She and Eddie often gave concerts around the parishes in the Diocese. The family had great hopes for both of them in music, but Eddie had other ideas. He wanted above all else to be a Catholic priest. Like Samuel in the Old Testament, he was called by God at an early age.

The big game was scheduled for the Saturday after the retreat that marked the beginning of the academic year. Time for recreation was allowed during the retreat and Pop O'Brien approached Jeff Collins, who had been an outstanding football player at West Catholic in Philadelphia. Jeff was made first team "'All Catholic" and second team "All State". Jeff had desired to enter the Diocesan Seminary in Philadelphia, but his uncle who was a Priest in the Midwest persuaded him to come to his Diocese. Pop O'Brien liked Jeff's style right away. "We got a kid from Philly who was an outstanding football player. He can hit a baseball a country mile," Pop said to Fr. Garrity. "I'll be there, Pop, cheering the new guys on," responded Fr. Garrity. Pop asked Jeff to get a team up and practice a little during recreation. "Remember, Jeff, we need ten guys. You know in softball they have a short fielder," Pop said. Jeff found seven players and including himself and Fr. O'Brien it made nine. He reported this to Fr. O'Brien, who told him to pick up some guy, even if he can't play well. Jeff tried to persuade some of the new students to join, but he couldn't find anyone who was willing. Eddie too was asked but emphatically refused. Fr. O'Brien went directly to Eddie and urged him to play. "It's not a big deal, kid, all you got to do is stand there and we'll back you up," Pop said while squeezing Eddie's arm. Against his better judgment Eddie agreed to play. "Good, kid, good kid," Pop said and raised a thumbs up gesture to Jeff who was standing nearby.

On the day of the big game, Eddie got the time mixed up and arrived late. Pop O'Brien was fuming. "Where were you, Eddie, we're waiting," he shouted. Eddie noticed that there were one hundred upper classmen who were sitting on the grass to cheer the teams on. They flipped a coin and the new guys lost. They had to bat first. In the first inning Jeff Collins and Pop O'Brien each hit home runs to give the new guys an early lead. When the new guys took the field in the bottom of the first inning, Eddie took his place behind second base without a mitt. "Where's your mitt, Eddie, for crying out loud," Pop hollered and a cheer went up from the side lines. Someone ran out and gave Eddie a mitt at which there was another cheer. A seminarian on the side lines decided to give Eddie a ribbing. "Come on, Eddie, do your thing." Then a chorus began to chant, "Eddie, Eddie, Eddie." Eddie was absolutely mortified and would have crawled into a rabbit hole, if there had been one close by. Unfortunately, the first batter hit a scorching line drive straight at Eddie who simply stepped aside. The ball rolled between the out fielders and into the pond for a home run. A roar of laughter rose from the gallery. "Eddie, Eddie," they yelled in unison. Jeff, who was playing short stop, moved Eddie to short left field for a right handed batter. Another line drive landed at Eddie's feet, and again he jumped aside. Applause from the crowd erupted again.

Eddie was batting number ten. "Drill it, Eddie, knock it out of the park, put it in the pond," someone shouted and everyone laughed. Eddie whiffed on three pitches. During the game Eddie struck out two more times. On the fourth time at bat, Eddie hit a grounder right to the pitcher, who ran over and tagged him out to the amusement of all. In the ninth inning the new guys were winning ten to nine. Jeff and Pop had a discussion. Since all three batters were right handed, they decided to put Eddie in right field and move the right fielder in to cut off line drives to left field. The only problem with this idea was that with slow pitching a good batter could place the ball any place he liked. The first batter hit a line drive down the third base line and easily got to second base. The next batter put his right foot back and aimed for right field. A high blooper was heading for Eddie. Eddie was standing in water up to his knees as the ball floated toward him. Instinctively, he backed up and stuck out his glove. The ball landed right in his mitt. For an instant it seemed that Eddie had caught the ball. But, no, Eddie stumbled and fell back into the pond and went under water. The ball was seen floating on the water. "Throw it here, Eddie, throw it here," Jeff yelled. Eddie retrieved the ball and threw it under hand to Jeff who whirled around and threw a perfect strike to the catcher in the hope of nailing the second runner at home. The runner slid under the catcher's glove and was called safe. Eleven to ten, the "World" had won. Some upper class men ran out and put

Eddie on their shoulders and carried him to home plate while all were chanting, "Eddie, Eddie." Eddie turned and saw that Pop O'Brien and Jeff Collins had buried their heads in obvious disappointment. Eddie made a "V" sign to no one in particular and dejectedly walked away. It was one of the lowest points of Eddie's life. Anyone who witnessed that event stored it in their memory. In later years when they met Eddie, they would say, "Eddie Lewis, yeah, I remember you. Aren't you the one who………………"

Old Jimmy Garrity was on a walker now, but fortunately he could maneuver himself to the podium where Fr. Lewis was gathering up and putting the music score into his brief case. "Eddie, you were magnificent. I'm so proud," said Jimmy as he shook Eddie's hand. "My goodness," responded Eddie, "Fr. Garrity, my old mathematics professor from the seminary. How are you, Father?" Eddie gave Father Jimmy a big abrazo and answsered, "Hangin' in there, Eddie. Hangin' in there," Jimmy said with tears in his eyes. "I was so proud of you today, Eddie, so proud. I couldn't help remembering that famous soft ball game when you were a first year student." Jimmy continued. "You've got a good memory, Father. I was hoping that that game would be forgotten completely," Eddie said with a smile. "I felt like a first class boob out there, and even though the ribbing was in all good fun, I was hurt by it all. Pop O'Brien and Jeff Collins were so disappointed when I fell back into the lake and lost the ball. I swore I'd never play again and never did." "Well, Eddie Lewis has come a long way since that day. Just think. You directed the choir at the Mass for the Pope himself. Who could ask for more?" Jimmy said, while wiping his eyes with a tissue. Eddie stopped and got very solemn. "Jimmy, it's a big secret but Jeff Collins is Cardinal elect. Tomorrow in the Observatore Romano they are going to list the new cardinals. Jeff is one of them who will get a red hat. Isn't that something?" "No kiddin," said Jimmy, "That's great. Jeff was such an outstanding student. We sent him to Rome for his Doctorate. Just think. You and Bishop Collins are from the same class." "Yeah," answered Eddie, "Pop O'Brien would be proud of us. A slob and a pro both made good." Eddie Lewis and Jimmy Garrity walked toward the elevator. Eddie was smiling with great satisfaction. His greatest game was finally behind him.

The Life and Times of Fr. Frank Donovan

After Pete Donovan returned from France in 1918, he went back to O'Leary's cabinet maker's shop to resume his apprenticeship. No one knew exactly where Eamon O'Leary, the head of the shop, had learned the trade since he avoided the topic like the flu. Eamon suggested, "You're welcome back, Pete, but I can't teach you anymore than you already know. Why don't you start up a business on your own? I'll back you with a no interest loan." Pete Dovovan advertised in the parish bulletin for a place where he could set up a shop. An answer came that evening at a bar. "I'll give you a shop and some tools for free on the condition that you hire my brother, Franny, who has been in trouble with the law for drinking and brawling," Benedict Mullin said over a pint. "It's no use kicking his butt, because he's as stubborn as a mule. The more you hound him, the nastier he gets. But those are the conditions. Take them or leave them." "I'll take them, Ben, and will welcome your brother, Franny. I'll keep him busy and help him to learn the trade," Pete replied. Pete and Franny worked together for weeks on a new cabinet. Pete wanted it to be a model for future sales. Franny was quick to learn and when he dated Eileen Kearns, he settled down. Franny and Eileen went to dances in the church basement where chaperones kept a stern eye on the youth. Pete wanted to be financially secure before he looked for a wife (not that he wasn't interested). He showed off his perfectly designed cabinet in front of the church. Fr. Eugene (Gene) Conroy mentioned it at the announcements after Mass. "There's a beautiful cabinet made by our doughboy, Pete Donovan. It's up for bids. I hope you outbid me. Be careful, you'll have bad luck for the rest of your life if you don't outbid a priest," Fr. Conroy said jokingly. The parishioners were very favorable in their judgment of Pete's talents and his integrity. The cabinet went for ninety dollars, after Fr. Conroy dropped out of the bidding. Not only that, but he also received requests for less expensive cabinets along the line of the one he presented at the church. "I could hack fifty bucks," one of the parishioners remarked. In two months Frank sold five cabinets, and he was pleased that he was building a reputation. He counted Franny's hours of work and paid him with his new income.

After that, he was ready for the "search" (as he called it). He wanted a bride, but he was determined to study all prospects so that he wouldn't get a "nagger" and/or a "yakker" (as he told Franny after work one day). When he attended the parish dance, the young people had their first names pinned to their shirts and blouses so that a fellow or girl who was shy could ask for a dance. Pete stood at the table where punch was served, and in his bashfulness, he just stared at the floor as if he were a lost child. After all, he was four or five years older than the young people attending the dance. On the other side of the room, Pete saw a girl as equally apprehensive as he. He took a long swig of punch and walked slowly to the girl. She had the name "Rose" pinned to her blouse. "If you're from Tralee, I'll ask you to dance," Pete said in a timid way. "I'm not from Tralee, I'm from Brooklyn, but my father is. That's why he called me Rose," she answered with a smile that melted Pete's heart. "Franny's my cousin and told me that you don't like women who are "yakkers" or "naggers." With four girls in my family, my Dad always says, 'Cripes, I can't get a word in edgewise' My Mom isn't a nagger, but she runs everything. She gives orders like a sergeant in the army. Kate, the eldest in the family, got married to a farmer. Elise, the second oldest, is searching frantically for a boyfriend and Annie, just above me, is going to nursing school, where the Nuns watch the students carefully. Franny said that you might like me even though I'm a "yakker," but I would never be a "nag," she said in one breath and then took another deep gasp. It seemed for a moment that she would continue this monologue. But Pete broke in and said, "You're the loveliest 'yakker' I've ever met. Would you like to dance with me?" They both laughed. Pete was instantly smitten by this vivacious, pretty girl. His "search" ended before it even got started. Pete won Rose's parents over by giving them a cabinet that he and Franny had assembled. Before long, he went to dinner with the family every Sunday evening. He was concerned about his own age, twenty four, compared to Rose's age, 18. "Rose is a great kid, Pete, she'll talk your ear off, but she has good horse sense, a touch of wisdom," her Dad said not in flattery, but from his deep confidence in his loving daughter. Pete proposed on Rose's nineteenth birthday. Fr. Conroy prepared them for the big step with his sage advice. After the marriage ceremony, Pete and Rose went to Florida on their honeymoon, and talked at length about the family they both wanted.

Four children were born to them, and Rose proved to be a loving, but strict mother and Pete an industrious and caring father. The financial crash in nineteen-twenty-nine took away the family's income. The cabinet business didn't have a chance when people could barely buy food. Pete asked Fr. Conroy if he could be a handyman in the church. Fr. Gene already had one caretaker, but decided to hire Pete also and pay him out of his own money. Rose took in laundry and she and Frank, her eldest son, would pick up and deliver laundry in a big bamboo basket that Pete had made. Frank was only seven years old, but he took his chores seriously and loved walking with his Mom, whom he loved very much. She would talk constantly back and forth to their clients. Often, they would say the rosary together. Once when they returned from a delivery, Franky (as he was called) told his Dad, "mommy talked the whole time." Pete rolled his eyes and said, "that's why we love her." Rose came over and kissed Pete on the forehead. The family made it through the depression and even sent the children to parochial school which was free at the time. Rose would take vegetables and bread to the Nuns, where she learned that Franky was "a good kid." Franky loved his second grade teacher, Sr. Mary Catherine, who remained loyal to him, even after he went off to war. His sisters and baby brother barely remembered anything from before the war, but Franky remembered his Dad cutting grass in front of the church and delivering laundry with his Mom.

In nineteen-thirty-eight, he entered the Jesuit run Regis High School. He worked part time at night in a pharmacy and during the summers he caddied. After graduating from high school in 1942, he was conscripted and sent to an Air force base in North Carolina. When he finished basic training he was sent to a base, where they prepared the young men in various capacities to go on bombing missions. Frank was asked what he'd like to do and before he could answer, the sergeant said, "Yeah, you'll make a good bombardier, private. Thanks for volunteering." At the base he learned how to drop bombs. In early 1944, he was sent to England to begin a period of bombing missions. Bobby "Spook" Jensen was the pilot with long experience. He was nicknamed "Spook," because he was shot down over France. With the help of the underground, he was able to make his way back to England. "Spook" was reluctant to go on any more missions, but he was ordered to return to duty. Frank Donovan was his bombardier. On the first three missions, they lost four gunners and took a lot of flak, which riddled the plane's frame. On their fourth mission they were shot down over Germany. Spook had his crew bail out, but before he could get to the door himself, the plane exploded. Frank and two of the crew were captured by German soldiers as they hit the ground. At that time, Frank, didn't know that he was listed as killed in action, to the great sorrow of his family. A memorial Mass was said for him, and the faculty at Regis hung his picture on the wall with a gold star under it.

In the prison camp a strict line of command was preserved. This was a well proven strategy to keep up morale and to do chores in a regulated manner. On their own, they did not salute each other for fear that the guards would single out those in authority. A captain kept repeating to the young flyers, "don't listen to rumors or you'll go bananas." In nineteen-forty-five the prisoners of war realized that the allies were approaching. Everyone was terrified that the Germans might shoot them. One morning there was no horn to get them out of bed. When they went out into the assembly field, they noticed that all the guards had vanished. After two days, American tanks could be seen on the hill overlooking the camp. The tanks slowly approached, and after observing that there were no guards on the premises, soldiers, with fixed bayonets, appeared from behind the tanks. To the prisoners' surprise, these soldiers seem to be Asian. Soon they found out that they were an elite group of Japanese Americans. There was complete pandemonium, as the prisoners realized that they were now free. Red Cross trucks arrived and gave them food, new clothing and sweets. When Pete called home, his younger sister, Rosie Marie, answered. "Hello, this is Frank," he said and the girl answered, "Frank who?" Rose took the phone and wept for a long time, "We thought you were dead and we even had a funeral Mass for you." Frank was mustered out of the Army in January nineteen-forty-six. His dad, Pete, was overcome and cried into his handkerchief, "We thought we had lost you. We thought we had lost you." Rose hugged him for a long time and whispered in his ear, "Welcome home, soldier. Welcome home, Franky." Frank met his siblings who had grown up into strong young people. Rose Marie (Rosey) Patricia (Patty), and Pete Jr. (who was called "brat" by his older sisters) all hugged him.

Frank Donovan had already decided to become a priest. He had met and was impressed by some chaplains in the Air force, who were either diocesan or religious order priests. He was attracted to the Dominicans and the Maryknollers, but old Fr. O'Leary badgered him into entering the New York Archdiocese. He entered Dunwoody, the seminary for the diocese, moved along in his studies and was ordained a priest in his home parish in nineteen-fifty-two. His first Mass and breakfast were very touching. When he gave Rose and Pete his first blessing, he felt a joy that was so deep that he could never express it. When Rose hugged him again, this time, she whispered, "if you become a chaplain for the boys in Korea, I'll never forgive you." "Don't worry, Mom," Pete retorted, "I had my fill of the service."

Frank served in various parishes in the archdiocese and, because of his background and maturity, he was well respected. He refused adamantly to discuss his war experiences. He took to drinking martinis with the pastor and the other associate pastors (at that time, three assistant priests in one parish was not unusual). He made many priest friends and was always close to his class mates from Dunwoody. They had been told many times during their formation that nourishing good friendships with other priests was one of the keys to a happy life. Frank found that that was excellent advice.

On his tenth anniversary as a priest, his class mates from Dunwoody had a con-celebrated Mass and then went out to dinner. The conversation centered upon the word "lavender" as applied to some seminaries throughout the country. Stories were told of a few young priests who were weird, and Frank was astounded to learn that some priests were flaunting ear rings and leather jackets. It wasn't unusual, he learned, for some priests to go to gay bars and spas. As a tough old soldier, Frank considered these trends to be disconcerting. "These are strange times, man," one priest said at a poker game.

The Cardinal asked Frank to consider taking over a parish in a poor section of the city, which was losing the immigrants who had settled there. The Cardinal explained that the church was run down, but that the school was still open, thanks to the sacrifices of the Dominican Sisters who worked only for their upkeep and did not receive a pension or insurance. There were drug trafficking and violence in the neighborhood. This would be a new venture for Frank, and after a period of discernment, Frank decided to give it a try. When he met his first group of black Catholics, he was astounded at their deep faith and trust in God. They were deeply indebted to the Sisters, who they said, made the school into a family atmosphere. The children flourished there and went on to high school and college. The graduates had done extremely well in society. "The public schools are punk," they said. "Imagine having cops patrol the corridors!" Through the school, many Protestant families became Catholic. The black families dolled up for the church services and the children wore bow ties or white dresses. Since the Church was allowing married Deacons, Frank asked two trusted men to take the two year course to become Deacons. They both were superb preachers in the black church tradition. Women in white dresses formed a choir and they all celebrated with joy. The Mass took an hour and a half, and the parishioners stayed after Mass to drink coffee and eat doughnuts. Two off-duty policemen were very visible at the bingo games, and the visitors from all over the city felt safe.

From the time of the Irish and Italian immigrants, there was an enormous parking lot, which was run down because of the small numbers of parishioners. Frank suggested to the parish council that they make the parking lot into two outdoor basketball courts with lights to play throughout the year. Frank went to the Cardinal and asked for a loan. The Cardinal agreed and gave the parish enough funds to build the courts at two percent interest over ten years. Frank also placed benches, so that the families could come and applaud for their kids. The boys had one court and the girls the other. The youth formed teams, played each other every night and there was a tournament every weekend. This policy of basketball proved to be successful, and fans came from all over to watch some potential stars. There were two players from Villanova University who came and worked with the youth during summer vacation. The elders of the parish took up collections after each game and sold candy and juice made cheaply from powder. Some of the high school kids were already playing in their own schools. So the level of basketball was very high. Players from college would ref the games and became role models. Again, off duty policemen watched the crowd in order to ward off trouble. No alcohol or drugs were permitted around the courts. Frank would ref some games too. Basketball brought in some income and was especially good for the neighborhood.

An elderly retired priest, Fr. Damien McDonough, lived with Frank in the rectory, but because of a stroke, he rarely left his room except to say Mass and take his meals. Frank kept the rectory and church under lock and key and had bright lights all around the property. Even though his family tree was riddled with alcoholics, he continued his custom of drinking martinis. Frank thought he could handle it. He was extremely indignant, when he was reported to the Cardinal for being tipsy at Mass. The Cardinal advised him to go to the Guest House in Milwaukee, where priests who were addicted to alcohol or drugs could get rehabilitated. When Frank finally admitted openly that he was an alcoholic, he began on the road to recovery. He returned from this therapy and was given a room in the Cardinal's house, while he awaited a transfer to another parish. His younger brother, Pete, had returned from Vietnam with no bodily wounds, but with a troubled spirit and often fought with his parents. He worked in the shop with his Dad, but they didn't communicate very well. He did make a comeback, when he dated and later married Gina Barcini, a first generation Italian girl who was very mature and desired a family. She had strong bonds to her own family. Instantly, Rose and Pete loved her.

In 1972 Frank Donavan was a priest for twenty years. He settled into an affluent church in Scarsdale and his parishioners were well educated, bright and savvy. They gave him prudent and excellent advice. They were very respectful and tended to be conservative in politics with ties to the Republican Party, in contrast to the people in the poor areas who were die-hard Democrats. In his conversations with women, he kept hearing the word "feminism." He asked the secretary of the parish what THAT meant. She informed him, with some vehemence, that it was the era when women took their rightful place in society and were struggling for equal rights. His mother, Rose, was bitterly opposed to these trends. "Yeah," she said, "try and look for the words 'motherly' or 'the joy of motherhood' and you will never find them. Raising children is a full time job. Abortion rights are anti-feminine. How could a mother kill her child?" Catholic women were also divided along the lines of secular society. Then more and more he had confrontations on this subject of "feminism." Pete read an article in the newspaper that some women were advocating women priests. The Nuns he knew in grammar school were different from these Sisters who were well educated, theologically astute and strong-minded. At poker games, feminism was often a topic. He heard different stories about THESE Nuns who were compared to the ones they knew in their childhood. Rose met a Nun at the hair dressers who was very articulate. Pete, ever the quiet observer, said, "it's a new era. Like it or not, women's rights are the wave of the future. Why can't we have women priests? I don't see any problem." American society, itself deeply divided politically and culturally impacted on the Church, which became equally divided along the same lines. It was almost an insult to use the words "conservative" or "liberal", when speaking of another Catholic's point of view.

During the eighties and nineties, "trickle down" economics of President Reagan was a big topic on television round tables. Reagan and Pope Paul II were able to bring down the "evil empire". Oil prices, recessions, danger in the Middle East were all troubles on the horizon. Pete died in nineteen eighty and had a big funeral. Rose was crushed. The families of Rosey, Patty and Pete Jr. all attended the funeral. Pete Jr.'s elder son did the first reading and Rosey did the second. Frank stumbled through the Mass and cried all through the homily. They had a catered lunch after returning from the cemetery. Rose remained in the old homestead, learned how to drive a car and went out to lunch with her "red hatter" friends. "That Lizzy can keep three conversations going on at the same time. I couldn't get a word in," she would say, knowing all the time that Lizzy was saying the same thing about her. Rose grew increasingly forgetful and voluntarily entered an old folks' home run by Nuns. "They got Mass every week and Fr. Riley is very nice," she would say, until the time when because of Alzheimer's disease she couldn't recognize anyone. It was a sad time for everyone. Rose died in her sleep, when she was ninety years old. Quiet Pete and loquacious Rose, the two love birds, finally were together again.

During the nineties, Frank was recognized as a leader in the Archdiocese and was elected twice to be president of the priests' senate. He continued to minister in many parishes throughout the Archdiocese. In twenty thousand and two, Frank celebrated his fiftieth anniversary to the Priesthood, and to his surprise, his sister, Rosey, invited his friends from various parishes where Fr. Frank had served. About thirty black Catholics and people from other parishes attended the Mass and celebration in St. Isaac Jogues church in Brooklyn. At the reception, Rosey invited the guests to recall some episodes from their experiences with Fr. Frank. It was the height of the abuse crisis, but his friends told touching stories about this highly respected priest. A gunner from his squadron was there and related how they had been prisoners of war together and how joyful they were to see the American tanks approaching the prison camp. All applauded at this story which was unknown to most of them. A black woman related how she had played basketball on the church's courts and had received a scholarship to Iona College. Pete Jr., now a grandfather himself and president of a cabinet makers' company, gave a toast to a "good priest who has seen everything. God bless you, Fr. Frank," he said. Since Franny Mullin had passed away, his wife and family attended the Mass and dinner. Within that year, Fr. Frank Donovan was diagnosed with brain cancer and died on his eightieth birthday. The Veterans of Foreign Wars attended his funeral. The flag on his coffin was removed and given to Rosie just before he was laid to rest next to his Mom and Dad. Rosey gave out cards with a picture of young Frank Donovan in his flight jacket with his crew. Indeed, Fr. Donovan had seen everything. He had survived the depression and the Second World War, became a priest, lived through continuous wars, none of which he supported, a Catholic president who was assassinated, the fall of the Russian Empire, the Second Vatican Council with all the changes in the Liturgy, the Church triumphant in the sixties to the disheartened Church in his later life, the abuse crisis, the relentless attacks on the Church by the media, and the insulting jokes by comedians. Fr. Frank had lived within the twentieth-century with all its events on the world stage. In the Church, he had a long history of priestly ministry, where he carried out his duties in humility and faith. It was true. Fr. Frank Donovan had seen everything. The tomb stone that the family placed over the plot where Fr. Frank had been laid to rest, read: "Fr. Frank J. Donovan. Loyal Patriot and Faithful Priest, 1922–2002." It was a great tribute to Fr. Frank Donovan and summed up his life perfectly.

Padre Gregorio's Guardian Angel

Fr. Gregorio Falcone was an Italian Franciscan priest who was born in Salerno in 1924 and died in Hong Kong in 1994. His parish priest sent many young boys to the Diocesan, Religious Orders and Congregations. Gregorio was only thirteen years old, when he entered the Franciscans (OFM) in Sicily. His parents were very fervent Catholics, who belonged to the Third Order Franciscans.

His mother did the linen for the church, among other chores she performed there. His father was killed in the bitter battle of Salerno, when the allied forces moved through Sicily. He had been an affectionate husband and father. He had worked in the City Office and would often joke, "There are no bureaucrats like Italian bureaucrats." His mother was an expert in preparing Pasta and was very strict with the children's studies. In the evening, when the children were studying, she sat in a rocking chair while knitting, and observed them. One of his brothers, Francesco, became a physician and his sister, Julia, joined a Congregation of Nuns who ran hospitals. When Gregorino (little Gregory) asked if he could enter the Franciscans, the family was delighted. Padre Guiseppe who had baptized Gregory, said to his parents, "I knew he had a vocation from the day he was born."

Gregorio thrived in the minor seminary and never wavered in his vocation, even though many students dropped out after finishing high school. By entering the minor seminary with no intention of continuing on to the priesthood, some poor children misused the system to obtain a good and free education. The seminaries at the time desired to get young boys before they went to work. It wasn't a perfect system, but many fine young men became Friars and went on to carry out outstanding ministry.

In 1947, he was ordained in the Naples' Cathedral. Padre Gregorio returned to his native city, Salerno, which had been reduced to rubble. At his First Mass, an elderly Padre Giuseppe gave a long and emotional homily on Padre Gregorio's loving family, his strong personality and the joy of the priesthood. At the end of the Mass, Padre Gregorio, after thanking his family and friends, mentioned that someday he would like to go on the missions, preferably China. In 1948 Padre Gregorio sailed for Shanghai where he began intense studies of the Chinese language. It was the fulfillment of his dream since early childhood.

The study of the language took place in the Franciscan Mother House in Shanghai and continued on over a period of two years. There were three private teachers, who took turns during the day to approach the language from various angles. On the very first day, he was introduced to the written language, by which he gained insight into Chinese culture and history. In his second year, he was initiated into the maxims of Confucius. He was impressed with the beautiful Chinese poetry which reflected the deepest feelings of the Chinese people.

Mrs. Chang, a very strict teacher of reading, made him prepare texts for the following day. She would scold him, "To be on a par with the Mandarins, you'll have to have a high level knowledge of Chinese literature. Right now you're far behind the pace of the Jesuits I taught." The teacher of spoken language required laborious repetition in mastering the tones. The same word could have different meanings according to the inflection. He had written tests every day, once a week, once a month, and a final in which all the symbols he had learned during the semester were included. Gregorio could hardly keep up the pace. He wasn't intimidated by Mrs. Chang, even though she never praised him. She stopped comparing him to the Jesuits. Eventually all three of his teachers were shot by the communists, because of their fraternizing with foreigners.

In the evenings Gregorio would visit the enormous outside markets where everything, even edible snakes, were sold. The women in charge would give him fruit and talk to him while carrying out their chores. He would continually misspeak the intonations and he would never forget their comment about it, "What's THAT you're saying?" It would be part of his conversations in later years, when he couldn't understand someone.

During his language training, Gregorio would sometimes travel by himself to visit a compound north of Shanghai, where an Italian Franciscan Bishop, Stefano Spada, resided. The trip involved sleeping out two nights because wandering bandits were everywhere. The high walls around the compound served as a protection from them. Four Passionist priests were killed by them, when their van got stuck in the sand.

Bishop Stefano was a brilliant expert on Chinese culture, besides being a jolly raconteur of his own experiences. The Bishop would tell all the young missionaries, "if you don't like the Chinese people, go home, NOW. You'll never be happy. The Chinese have a sixth sense of discerning whether the missionary really has affection for them." The Bishop knew from Gregorio's file that he was a good, but overly serious Friar. "Hey, Gregorino (little Gregory), lighten up. You can only make it here if you have an sense of humor." The Bishop was quite pleased about Gregorio's progress in the language, especially with the tones. As his studies came to a close, Gregorio was happy to leave Shanghai where the hatred between the foreigners and the Chinese caused unbreakable divisions which eventually would lead to revolution.

They despised each other. The infamous sign in a park in Shanghai which read: "Dogs and Chinese keep out" was well known, not only in Shanghai, but also throughout the entire country. The intrigue, treachery and debauchery in Shanghai, before the communists took over, left a deep scar of cruelty on the collective memory of the Chinese people. They would return that cruelty in the coming revolution.

After graduating from language school, Padre Gregorio's first assignment was to the Bishop's compound where Mass was offered, many confessions were heard, and the care for the sick and homeless was carried out. Gregorio was put in charge of three groups of the Legion of Mary which flourished at that time. The members (soldiers) of the Legion instructed catechumens and prepared them for Baptism. Every year at Easter as many as a hundred catechumens were baptized. Bishop Stefano demanded that those who were preparing for Baptism study for at least two years. The last six months of their preparation was handled by the Bishop himself. Those who were not ready for Baptism were held up for another year. The members of the Legion also taught Catholic children catechism. Some children would bring their non-Christian friends to catechism class, many of whom were baptized in later years.

Accompanied by guards, Padre Gregorio would often visit Catholics who lived outside the compound. He would deliver food and medicine to the leaders of the villages and ask them to distribute these items not just to Catholics, but to anyone who was in need. The leaders were observed carefully by the women so that the provisions were shared equally. Gregorio also formed more groups of the Legion of Mary to care for the people who lived in the hamlets. When the Bishop would have an official visit to these small towns, he would quiz the catechumens to see if they were ready for Baptism. Then at Mass, he would baptize them. The flock in those areas increased beyond the Bishop's expectation.

The unstable political situation and the threat of communist intrusion put fear into the people. From Sicily, the Provincial of the Franciscans urged the Bishop and the Friars to flee from the communists. Even Bishop Stefano spoke at length with them about this. At first, many Friars refused to go. When the Bishop saw this, he ordered them all to leave except Gregorio. "I want you to help me discern how to deal with the Communists and save as many Christians as possible." Padre Gregorio, with his mastery of the language, his dedication and unflappability, he thought, would be a great aid in the event of a crisis. In 1952 the communists did come.

At first, both the Bishop and Gregorio were called in for questioning. They were held overnight and ordered to write their life history. Then for a time they were released and forbidden to leave the compound. The Bishop cautioned Gregorio that his life history was one of the sources that the well prepared interrogators would use to torment him, and try to break his spirit. The Bishop cautioned him, "Write the same story every time and don't divulge anything of your personal life that could be used against you." This proved to be excellent advice when, eventually Gregorio was imprisoned. After two years of house arrest, the Bishop was deported to Italy, and he and Gregorio would never meet again. Evidently, Gregorio's connection to the Legion of Mary was the chief reason he was imprisoned. To his sadness and discouragement, he was informed by the warden which members of the Legion had been executed. The communists considered these small groups of Christians, who met together privately, as the greatest threat to their regime.

Bound hand and foot, Gregorio was taken by truck to the infamous prison in Shanghai. The prisoners slept on the floor and were given a large metal cup which was used both for eating and for hygienic purposes. During the period of orientation, the prisoners were forced to memorize the regulations as well as the rules for appropriate behavior in the confinement area. At the morning assembly, the prisoners were made to shout out these rules in unison. During private interrogations, they had to recite the precepts again. The Chinese inmates completely avoided Gregorio for fear that they would be punished for fraternizing with a foreigner. His isolation had begun.

After Gregorio was separated from the other prisoners, the ordeal of writing his life story began. He tried to remember what he had written before and to write exactly the same thing. For the first week, all his notes were ripped up in front of him. They would then slap his face back and forth, and tell him that he was lying. Gregorio would change only insignificant things, such as the time he spent in the minor seminary and other non-essential things. The questioners would pounce on any discrepancies and question him at length on these points. Gregorio would try to justify himself by saying, "Well, I must have gotten that mixed up again." He would get another slap in the face and be sent back to his cell. The temptation to say something personal during these sessions was always there. Gregorio fought these off by constant prayer. When he was commanded to write about his family, he would give only nebulous answers. Once the officer in charge punched him in the stomach and slapped him. "Tell me about your relations with your mother. Did she love you? Did she have a cold personality? Did she favor your siblings over you? Write that down and don't lie," the officer shouted again and again. Gregorio gave vague answers only to get a punch in the stomach and a slap in the face in return. In a fit of anger, he responded, "Why do you keep asking about my mother? Didn't your mother love you?" At this, the interrogator knocked him off his chair and began to pummel him. Gregorio felt that he would die until the interrogator was pulled off him and never returned.

After six months of torture, Gregorio was put in solitary confinement twenty three hours a day, with one hour outside for exercise. He had to sit in a squatting position.

The guards could observe him from an invisible peep hole. Whenever he fell asleep, the guards would come in, beat him and cuff his hands behind his back. This was the worst trial of all. If he spilt his tea, his thirst until the next day was almost unbearable. Once when he dropped his tea cup, he fell over on his side and began to weep without restraint. "Oh, God help me," he prayed, "I cannot endure much more." He just lay there choking and crying. "Help me, God, do not abandon me," he repeated. The guards came in again and beat him. Gregorio slipped into deep despair. He must have nodded for a time, because when he awoke, he seemed to be having a hallucination. He heard the sound of a bird sounding like the song of a canary. The canary perched on his shoulder and sang in his ear. He reached out to catch it, but the bird flew all around the room and perched on a spot beyond the view of the guards. Eventually, it stopped singing and just stared at him. It began to nod its head up and down signaling a "yes." What could that mean? Could it mean that the guards were watching him? Gregorio sat still. The guards did not enter. Then the bird shook its head back and forth. Gregorio took this to mean that the guards were gone. Gregorio purposely closed his eyes, as if he were sleeping. No one entered his cell. Sometime later, the bird nodded up and down again and Gregorio sat straight with his eyes wide open. This way he entirely avoided punishment for sleeping. When it was time for the evening meal, a guard entered and removed his handcuffs. Gregorio could now eat and drink in peace. The canary was gone.

Every day, just after his morning ablutions, the bird appeared again and perched in the same spot. When Gregorio saw a "no" sign, he would relax and lie down. Then when he saw a "yes" signal, he would straighten up into the appropriate position. This happened every day for over a year. Not once was he disciplined. With the help of his Guardian Angel, Gregorio now knew he could make it.

One morning, to Gregorio's utter dismay, the canary did not appear. Gregorio became dreadfully afraid that his torment might begin again. In the afternoon, his cell door opened and he recognized the warden. The chief officer sat on the floor opposite him and offered him a cigarette. "You priests are sly guys. I knew all the time that you had some way to tell when you were being watched or not. We could never figure it out," he said with a stern face. "It was my Guardian Angel. God sent him to help me," Gregorio answered with a smile. The warden glared at him and said, "The illusion of God can do many strange things." "What do you mean by illusion?" Gregorio said. "Perhaps YOU are the one under illusion." At that, the warden laughed sarcastically, but then said in a quiet way, "I admire you, prisoner. I saw you praying every time I looked into your cell. You looked so peaceful. I thought perhaps that you had forgiven us. Doesn't it say you should in your Bible?" Gregorio responded with a smile. "It wasn't easy. God helped me to forgive. I have no feelings of hatred toward you, but I will pray for you that you will find God and achieve happiness." The warden looked at Gregorio for a long time and then lifted him up. He shook hands with the Padre he had come to admire.

Gregorio was escorted to the border near Hong Kong and was met by the Red Cross and his fellow Franciscans. He just smiled with happiness. He knew he would have to tell them about his Guardian Angel. He related the story later on to the community and wrote about it in a long letter to his superiors in Italy. He especially enjoyed relating the story to new missionaries who came to minister in Hong Kong. Along with that story, he admonished them, "The only way to make it in China is to have affection for the Chinese. They'll know it in a minute, if you don't."

At Padre Gregorio's funeral Mass in 1994, the Franciscan homilist, after telling the story of the Guardian Angel, said an interesting thing about him. "He was so serious in his younger days, but after his release from prison, he always smiled and loved to laugh at jokes. Over a glass of vino, he could even become jolly. He loved the Chinese people so much and never spoke ill of them." Padre Gregorio's body was cremated and his ashes were placed in the Monastery's columbarium in Hong Kong. He had spent his entire adult life in China and never returned to Italy.

Fr. Dan's Secrets

Fr. Danny Sullivan was considered by the priests of the Baltimore Archdiocese to be likable but a "real character." There were many tales about Fr. Danny's desperate attempts to keep secrets that involved him personally. His sister, Grace, who was a practicing psychologist, always said about him, "He's compensating for something, but I don't know what." Would-be psychologists among the clergy had their own ideas on Danny. One theory was that, since he was the youngest of six siblings, one of them might have swiped his chocolates when he was a baby or one of his brothers might have pinched his toys. Since Danny had served in many parishes in the diocese, everyone who knew him related hilarious anecdotes about his escapades. One of his most famous tricks was, after he went to a movie or a concert, he would go out of his way to cross over a river, tear the ticket into very small pieces and then throw them into the river. "Conceal your tracks," was the motivation for his private life. Even with his family and priest friends, he would be equally secretive and tried to give them as little information as possible. This led him to a career of fun and games.

After ordination, Danny was sent to a small parish in the city, where he was associate pastor with the affable Fr. William (Bill) Dunn, with whom he got along famously. Fr. Danny took his ministry very seriously and was especially dedicated to the sick. In fact, in every parish he served after that, he was well known and respected for visiting hospitals and elderly people in their homes. He had an extraordinary reputation for his zeal and compassion. In other words, Fr. Danny was a good priest. The only reason he would be manipulative was when he wanted absolute secrecy concerning his day off. He negotiated with Fr. Bill the terms of his free day. At that time in the seventies, days off for the clergy started in the morning and ended at twelve midnight. Fr. Bill agreed to allow Fr. Dan to start his free day from six in the evening until the following day at six PM. When Dan was leaving for his day out, he would shout up the stairs, "See ya, Bill." The next night at precisely one minute to six, he would appear, put his head into Bill's room and say, "I'm back, Bill," and go straight to his room. At table, Bill would try very hard to find out exactly what his associate did on his days off. Dan would answer, "I just visit Mom. You know, buy groceries, clean the house and take Mom out for a drive, things like that." Fr. Dan could maneuver better than an Admiral on an aircraft carrier.

The only problem with Fr. Dan's private life and his secrets was that inevitably he would be found out. For instance, one Sunday after Mass, two people, who were speaking loudly said, "Hey, Fr. Dan, I saw you at the cinema the other night," and "Fr. Dan, I hear you play golf a lot on your day off." These enlightening tidbits and others easily reached the ears of Fr. Bill, who relished questioning Dan. "I didn't know you played golf on your day off, Dan. What do you shoot, in the eighties?" Dan would stutter and give as vague an answer as possible, "Yeah, well, you know, Fr. McGroary from Philly sometimes challenges me. I cream him and take his dough" (which wasn't a lie, because they had played together a few times). "Where do you play, Dan?" the pastor would ask. To this, Dan would roll his eyes and say, "Yeah, well, you know, we play at various places." Fr. Bill would continue eating, take a sip of wine and ask, "I hear you like movies. Do you go frequently?" Dan would cough and answer, "Yeah, well, you know, actually I took my Mom to see one of those romantic flicks she likes. Beyond that….you know, I take in one when there's a good movie playing, and you'd have to go a long way to find a good one these days." Fr. Bill would gloat and tell his priests friends at poker of Dan's equivocations. They would answer, "He sure is secretive, but such a good guy. He would give you the shirt off his back." Actually, Fr. Dan went to the movies almost every month and played golf with Fr. Gerry Griffin of his own diocese. Dan was concerned, though, that he was seen by people. He was determined to go farther away, when he ventured out on his day off.

One of the great stories about Dan was when he thought of buying a cottage at the Jersey shore. He went through a real estate agent in Camden, and really emphasized to the man the absolute necessity of keeping it quiet. "Don't even tell your wife, got that?" he said in a very forceful voice. That night the agent told his wife about this weird priest from Baltimore who desired absolute silence on the deal he wanted. His wife paused a long time before raising her eyebrows and saying, "That couldn't be Fr. Dan Sullivan, could it? Gee, I knew a fellow from my class at St. James who joined the Baltimore diocese." The agent whispered, "Yeah, that's the fellow, Dan Sullivan. But promise me you won't tell a soul. Keep it quiet just like the priest's secret of confession." His wife said. "OHHH, I would never breathe a word of it. If he wants it kept secret, who am I to reveal it?" After dinner, she called three of her friends from her school days and told them about Fr. Danny Sullivan's new cottage in Avalon. One answered, "Ohhhh, is that so? My husband's friend at work has a cottage in Avalon. I'll tell him to look Fr. Sullivan up," her classmate answered. "No, no, no! Swear on a stack of Bibles that you won't repeat it. My husband would go bonkers." "Ohhh, of course not, 'zipper lips,' that's my middle name," was the classmate's answer. It wasn't long before the pastor, Fr. Bill, heard the rumor. At dinner, there was a long silence while Fr. Bill thought of the appropriate words to broach the subject. He broke the silence by asking in a very serious voice, "Hey, Dan, the rumor is that you're buying a cottage at the Jersey Shore. Is it just a rumor?"

"Where the heck did you hear that? Geez, I was just talking with an agent. But I'm not sure if I'll go through with it. Everybody seems to know it. Boy, there are no secrets in this world." The pastor just chuckled. That night the real estate agent got a very nasty phone call from Baltimore, "You promised, buddy, to keep our transaction a secret. Only you knew it. And now everybody from New York to Florida knows it. Well, I'll tell you something, buddy, our deal is off, off, off." That betrayal of confidence was the main reason that Fr. Dan decided to buy a cottage in North Beach on the Chesapeake Bay. On the day he moved in, he thought he would saunter down the boardwalk right along the beautiful bay. As he rambled along, in nifty khaki shorts and a Baltimore Ravens' tee shirt, to his surprise and disappointment, he met Jane and Tom Evans from the parish council. Dan returned to the cottage and had a long drink. There is nothing sacred, nothing, he thought. Fr. Bill, ever the raconteur, who heard of the North Beach transaction from Mrs. Evans, repeated at the priests' retreat the tale of the North Beach cottage, which spread like wild fire among the assembled clergy. More than being embarrassed, Dan was livid with anger and made up his mind that he would avoid the Evans' as much as possible. He really wasn't betrayed by the couple. It was just that they were the medium of letting the cat out of the bag.

A few weeks after this incident, the Cardinal called Fr. Bill to ask his advice on a personnel change for Fr. Dan. "With all due respect, your Excellency, I would love to keep Danny here. He's a heck of a good minister," answered the pastor. "Well, if you two get on well like that, I'll let him stay. I hear he's very secretive," the Cardinal replied. Dan was very happy to continue with Fr. Bill. He's very inquisitive, Dan thought, but a great pastor and a good friend.

Bill was ready to give Dan more responsibility in the parish. He asked Dan if he would mind being in charge of the CD program on Sundays. Dan agreed. Bill wasn't sure if Dan would like to take over the bingo program, but he voiced it anyway. "Sure, sure," Dan answered, "I'd be glad to do both, No problem at all." Bill continued, "Yeah, but there's one problem with the bingo. The income is way down. Maybe you could turn it around," Bill remarked. "I'll check that out, Father, and do my best," Dan responded with enthusiasm.

Sister Joseph Marie was in charge of the CD program and welcomed Fr. Dan into the group of teachers. After observing the schedule, materials and the teachers, he found out that there was a lot of repetition over the eight years. With input from Sister and the teachers, he tried to change the curriculum. He asked for a higher budget from Fr. Bill, who graciously agreed. He bought better materials, DVDs and an overhead projector. Sometimes, he also ordered hoagies or pizzas and soft drinks to take after class. Over the brunch, they would discuss their classes and make observations. This small lunch was paid from Dan's own pocket, so that no one would think that he was rifling the parish treasury on parties. At Christmas, he invited Fr. Bill, sister and the teachers out for dinner. Of course, no one knew about his special bank book, where he kept his stipends received from ministry. It wasn't a big deal, but the satisfaction of knowing that he had a secret bank account gave him great satisfaction.

Now, the bingo enterprise was a huge challenge. He attended all the evening bingos and often played himself. Since he refused any prizes, he never mentioned it when he won. If parishioners knew that a priest played alongside them, he thought, it might encourage more people to come. One evening after bingo, while he was watching television in his room, he heard the doorbell ring and went down stairs to open it. First, he glanced out the window to see who was there. Standing on the porch were a middle aged African American man and a Caucasian woman who appeared to be in her thirties. They both were impeccably dressed. When Dan opened the door, they both flashed FBI badges and said, "May we speak with Fr. Daniel Sullivan, plcase." "That's me. Come on in," Dan answered. They declined coffee and broke the ice by saying, "We're both Catholics, Father. The Bureau is full of us. Fordham graduates spy on CIA Harvard agents." Fr. Dan got the joke alright, but didn't laugh, he was so afraid. "Geez, I hope I didn't do anything wrong. When you flashed your badges, my knees started knocking," Dan mentioned in a quivering voice. "Don't worry, Father," the agent continued. "It's not about you, but we have infiltrated your bingo program and found that a few of your leaders are scooping some dough off the top. They have a system of passing the money under the table. You'd have to be very observant to witness them. Here are the names of the ones we spotted and have proof that they aren't on the up and up. We don't want to prosecute them, but we want you to remove them from your committee. If not, we'll book them." "I never realized," Dan responded in a quivering voice. "The pastor noticed that our income was down from before, but couldn't figure it out. Well, I'll take care of it. Count on that." "It happens all the time, Father," the younger agent related. As they approached the door to go out, the female agent turned to Dan and said with a smile, "By the way, Father, I hear through the grape vine that the IRS found out about your secret bank account. You ought to pay back taxes on that special fund." Dan put his hand on his brow, looked down sheepishly and apologized, "Gee, I'm real sorry about that. I forgot to put that account it into my taxes." The elder agent smiled and quoted Scripture, "There is nothing hidden that will not be revealed." Fr. Dan dismissed his bingo committee and cautioned them that the FBI was on their trail. They all registered at other parishes. After that, the income from Bingo rose dramatically to the joy of Fr. Bill. Without giving many details, Dan told his pastor that the FBI had visited him and gave him advice on how we might increase their winnings. It wasn't difficult for Fr. Bill to figure out what had happened, when he saw the new bingo committee. Bill filed the case in his brain for the future. "You can't be too careful, Dan," he said. "You can't be too careful."

A few months after this episode, Dan received another visitor. As he was making coffee in the kitchen for breakfast one morning, a knock came to the back door. As he glanced through the glass window on the door, he saw an elderly man, nattily dressed in dark clothing with white shoes. He was also sporting sun glasses. "Bad vibes" were Dan's first impressions. The guy looked like a gangster you see in the movies, he thought. The man smiled and blew smoke from his cigar at the window. Dan opened the door and asked the man who he was. "I'm Franco Angenelli. They call me 'angel' for short. Are you Fr. Dan?" The gentleman inquired. "Ah, yeah, that's me, of course, but why didn't you come to the front door?" Dan questioned. "Can I come in, Father, and talk to you before your secretary and cook come in at nine?" the man asked quietly. Dan invited him in and offered him coffee. The man nodded "Yes" and sat down at the kitchen table. He removed his glasses, asked for an ashtray for his cigar, just smiled at Dan for a long time and then said in a voice a little above a whisper, "This is just between you and me, Father, and I would ask for absolute discretion. Can I count on you?" "Discretion, that's me," Dan replied. While lighting another cigar, the man said, "Well, Father, let me put it this way. Someone who is very fond of you and hopes for your success in ministry asked me to talk to you about your bingo program. No offense, but you're a first class amateur at raising money. I don't know much, Father, but I DO know how people react to gambling. You've a nice, sedate layout, but, first of all, your prizes are too small. Who wants to come a long way to win twenty five or fifty bucks? With big prizes people have an incentive to come out at night. Why not offer one-thousand bucks for the last game of the night and then on Friday nights, you could offer three-thousand or something like that?" Fr. Dan gulped. "Another thing I'd like to suggest is a special night once a week or so. You could have seniors' nights, spouses' nights, young peoples' nights, old friends' nights, St. Patrick's night in March, Saint Anthony's night in June, and other types of nights, etcetera, etcetera. Use your imagination. That's why God gave you a brain. Big dough for prizes and some special reason to come out for a night, and you've got yourself a winner. They are the keys to making a bundle. I guarantee you, Father, this time next year Fr. Bill will be able to make the necessary renovations on the church and the school." At that, Angel stood up abruptly, relit his cigar, put on his sunglasses and hat, walked to the door, and stopped. Turning again to Fr. Dan, he said, "I'm giving you this advice, Father, at the request of a good friend of yours, who will remain anonymous. " Angel exited the door, walked across to the parking lot where a white limousine was waiting for him, and without looking back, he stepped into the car which drove off very quickly. Fr. Dan followed Angel's counsel if not to the letter at least he made some adventuresome changes, to the great concern of the new bingo committee who were as Dan said, "conservative." And, yes, they made a bundle. Fr. Bill was thrilled with the income from bingo. He was able to carry out the repairs that Angel had predicted. This, of course, did not go unnoticed. At the end of a priests' conference, the Cardinal singled out some of his priests to compliment them on some achievement. "And we can't forget Fr. Dan Sullivan, who proved to be a genius at raising funds. He has some kind of a secret method, which he won't reveal even to me. Maybe he has a little angel or something." When the Cardinal winked at him, Fr. Dan finally found out who his good friend was. It would always be his and the Cardinal's secret. A few days later, when the cardinal met with his council, he grinned and said, "Boys, we've got ourselves a trouble shooter."

Fr. Dan was made pastor far before many senior priests, (which did not go unnoticed). His first personnel change into the inner city was one of many he had in his career. He was sent to parishes, where they were facing financial difficulties. Dan's ingenuity at raising funds was as good as any broker on Wall Street. Even when bingo went out of fashion, Dan found other ways to put the parish on a firmer financial base. A few times after a review by the Cardinal's council, a school or church would be closed, but on the whole, Dan did a good job. "That guy's uncanny," one priest mentioned to his friend from seminary days. Dan's reputation went into orbit, and he often received phone calls from priests throughout the diocese, asking him to give them hints on raising money. Dan had a lot of secret methods that even Angel would admire. He released the most obvious, "Women are the ones you can count on. They are problem solvers just as in their households. After an affair is carried out, show your appreciation for them by taking them out for lunch. Women love lunches with their friends with no dishes to wash. They yak and yak, but you have to thank them profusely. Thanking volunteers really is the basis for future cooperation. Men are good also. Show you're appreciation by taking them out fishing or going to a ball game. While eating hot dogs and drinking beer, you just have to say, 'You guys are alright. I've never worked with a better group.' It's all common sense, you know, everybody likes to be appreciated." Even from the altar, Dan would praise the parishioners for their outstanding generosity after a drive to raise funds. "He's like someone who could sell ice to an Eskimo," one woman commented. To this remark, everyone was in agreement.

Fr. Dan would send out news letters to people, whose names he had garnered from some Catholic agencies. He learned through experience how to set up the letter. First of all, it had to be brief and to the point (he knew that people give up on long articles). Then, you have to tell the prospective donor exactly what you want. For instance, Dan would write, "I'd like to be able to permit poor children into the school. I could get along on about three-thousand-dollars a year per pupil. We charge tuition, but many children in our neighborhood cannot pay in full or can't pay at all. Education is a long time welfare plan that always ends in helping children achieve. You don't get immediate results on education, but it's the best investment I know to help indigent children. It's a great joy, when they go to college and make something of themselves in society." This type of letter was very effective. Donors usually gave small amounts, but sometimes he would make a big hit of five hundred or a thousand dollars.

The Chancery Office frequently asked Dan for his cell phone number, and Dan would answer vaguely, "Oh, yeah, sure, I don't have my cell phone with me now, but I'll get back to you." "Yeah, you always say that," the vicar responded, "suppose it's an emergency." The next day, Dan called in and gave his old cell phone number without revealing that he had just bought a more modern one with a new number. He gave the new number to his sister, Grace, but made her promise not to give it to anyone. This stratagem was devised so that he could disappear on his summer vacation without anyone knowing it. Of course, it backfired as usual. He and Gerry Griffin were staying in a Franciscan hostel in Nazareth and were on a tour by taxi to Caparnaum when he received an emergency call from Grace. "Shalom, Grace, what's happening?" he asked in a pleasant voice. Grace was sniffling and couldn't get the words out. "You're in big trouble with the chancery. Msgr. Burke has been trying to get you. Your parish church burnt down and they couldn't locate you with the number you gave them recently." "What do you mean, my church burnt down??" Dan answered in a very concerned voice. "It was late at night, thank God. It seems there was a short in your electric wires, the church burnt down before the fire engines could get there," she responded and started sniffling again. "Well, I'll come right back. If the Msgr. Burke calls again, let him know," Dan uttered in a very sad voice. The insurance covered everything, but he knew he had to rebuild. That is, until he met Msgr. Burke, the Vicar who with an angry red face said, "I'm fed up with your secret childish games. You are relieved of your duties in your present parish. I'll ask the Cardinal to give you another assignment when I get around to it." Dan was very embarrassed, because he had let the Cardinal down and fearful, because he had crossed Msgr. Burke whom he knew was someone that you didn't mess with. He wrote a very remorseful letter of apology to the Cardinal and expressed his respect for him and all that the Bishop had done for him.

After two anxious months, Dan received a call from the chancery office and told to report to the Cardinal the next day. He thought he would be scolded again and resolved to take any punishment he might receive. Dan was lead into the inner sanctum, where the Cardinal had his office. To Dan's utter amazement, who was sitting in a soft chair next to the Cardinal? It was none other than Msgr. Burke. "Dan, I got a job for you. Msgr. Burke here looked into one of our parishes and deduced that the pastor was a first class amateur (Dan remembered that these were the exact words Angel had used a few years ago). He informed me that you're the pro of the diocese", the Cardinal said, "and he recommends that you take over that parish." "Nobody's as good as you, Fr. Dan," the Vicar said. "You'll do fine there." Dan thanked the Bishop for his generosity and the Monsignor for his confidence. As Dan got up to leave, the Cardinal handed him a letter. It was Dan's letter of apology.

"Tear that up and throw it in the river," the Cardinal said. "I hear you donate a lot of your own money to helping poor kids." Dan was bewildered that his secret was known by the Cardinal. Dan as usual thrived in the new parish.

Years later, the Cardinal visited Dan in the hospital, when he had a severe stroke and his sister, Grace, was at his bedside. A young priest came in and gave Dan the sacred anointing of the Church. The Cardinal sat beside his bed too and said how proud everyone was of him and all that he had achieved during his career. Dan was unable to speak, but he signaled Grace with his eyes. She handed a letter to the Cardinal. "He wanted you to open it," Grace said. It was Dan's last will and testament duly signed by him and had the seal of the Notary Public. It read, "I give the house in North Beach to Grace. Any other funds that are left in my accounts, I give to the diocese. Please use it for a struggling parish." After a few minutes Fr. Dan died. It was Fr. Dan's last secret. "I wonder what other secrets he took to his grave," Grace said. "He was a heck of a trouble shooter" the Cardinal said, "but he sure enjoyed his secrets."

Father "Milky's" Legacy

The Bishop's secretary, Father Michael Hennesy, entered the Bishop's office and approached the desk where Bishop Thomas Hogan was seated. The young priest was carrying a brown envelope which seemed to be stapled in many places. "We went through Fr. Healy's effects as you advised, Your Excellency. We found nothing significant. He lived a rather simple life. There were classical records and some new CDs. It seems his pastime was classical music. He used ear phones, which indicate that he was thoughtful enough not to make noise that would annoy the other priests in the facility. We found some old books of Theology, which we put into the library. We found no kin. A twenty year old record of a cousin, who lived in Oregon was there in his desk. We called the phone number, but evidently it was changed many years ago. It was a dead end. Legally, he left everything to the diocese and his stocks and bonds were countersigned by our lawyer. There was an old faded chalice with the inscription that it was a gift from his parents. The date reflected that he had been ordained for over sixty years. There was a beautiful Russian Icon, which we placed in the chapel. And we found this brown envelope addressed to you. When it was written, we don't know. He was lucid and clear right up to the end. Since you were away when Fr. Healy died, I checked your schedule and designated next Monday for the Funeral Mass. I can change that if necessary. No problem. He has no family. The chapel in the Villa is always available."

Bishop Hogan listened carefully to what was said about this old priest who had died in his sleep at the Diocesan Villa. Fr. Joseph "Milky" Healy was a way before the Bishop's time, but he met Milky a few times when he visited the Villa. Fr. Healy was a good and gentle priest he remembered, very soft spoken and yet open, considering his old age. "So, Michael, how would you some up the life and times of Fr. Healy and why he was nicknamed 'Milky'?" the Bishop asked his trusted secretary. Fr. Hennesy answered with discreet language (he was a Canon Lawyer by profession and prudent by inclination). "Well, I went through his file that you gave me today and what I can gather is that he no bad marks against him, except in his early years as a priest some of his Pastors asked to have him changed. I take it there were chemistry problems. I noticed that he had never been nor requested to become a Pastor. One of those eternal associate Pastors who never rise to nor want to be a Pastor. Why, I don't know. Most priests are hands on guys who love nothing better than to change the place of the Tabernacle," (here they both chuckled). A nurse at the Villa, Eileen Muldoon, took care of him in his last days. Maybe she will know why he was called 'Milky'." "I have business at the Villa this afternoon and I'll talk to this nurse, Mrs. Muldoon," the Bishop said, as he stood up and shook hands with Fr. Hennesy. He placed the brown envelope on his desk without reading it.

Mrs. Muldoon was glad to speak with the Bishop. When she referred to Fr. Healy, she used the affectionate name "Milky." She explained, "at the time when Father Healy, Milky, was a seminarian the students were permitted to read the Sunday funnies. In one of the comic strips there was a character named Mr. Milktoast, who was clumsy, naïve and shy, the type who easily gets a ribbing because of their personality. Someone gave him the name Mr. Milktoast, which was later shortened to Milky. The name stuck to him like a fly to sticky paper. Fr. Healy resented the name very much, because it portrayed him as a wishy-washy patsy. He always said that true meekness could only be found in a person who had a very strong personality. Meek shouldn't mean weak is what he emphasized to me. He resented that nickname very much, but didn't seem to carry grudges or resentments. "

She continued, "Milky told me many stories of how he was abused by the take charge type pastors who ran roughshod over weak assistants. Some of his stories of his early years as a priest are actually hilarious. Once when he returned from a sick call at the hospital, the Pastor asked him how Elizabeth Jones was. He answered, 'Mrs. Jones'? 'Don't give me that stuff. You went to the hospital, right?' the Pastor answered showing signs of indignation. 'hospital? What hospital?' Milky would say very calmly. 'THE HOSPITAL you went to on a sick call. Are you pulling my leg, Buster?' Milky answered, 'Oh, yeah, the hospital. I went there this afternoon,' he would say as if everything was just dawning on him. The pastor's face would get red and he would start shouting, 'listen, Buddy, you'll be out of here in the morning on your backside and you better believe it.' As the pastor stomped out of the room, Milky would shout after him, 'Elizabeth was discharged yesterday.' The pastor would give him the silent treatment for two or three days. Milky always thought he could handle those hardnosed pastors."

"Another story he liked was about a pastor who felt he was competent to express his views on any subject. Milky rarely listened to him. Once when this Pastor was on the topic of Asian languages, he was keenly interested. 'Ya see, Milky, Asian languages are tonal. That means you can have the same sound like 'hu' and according to your intonation, the meaning of the word changes. It's a devil to get those eight tones down.' Well Milky, who was well read, said, 'Actually there are four tones in Chinese and neither Japanese nor Korean are tonal.' The pastor evidently exploded, brought his fist down on the table and said, 'don't you know, son, that China is the biggest country in Asia and CHINESE IS TONAL.' Milky knew that he had scored some points."

The nurse smiled and continued, "He was a Prince though, never complained. He loved classical music and could identify the composer and the part of the arrangement he was listening to. He was very cultured and extremely knowledgeable of literature. He never wanted to be a pastor. 'Goodness no, Eileen' he would say, 'upkeep of buildings, construction, repairs, a school, difficult parents, budgets and all that stuff. I was content to hear confessions, say Mass, visit the sick, teach catechism and lead the Legion of Mary. Many of the Pastors liked me for my loyalty to my pastoral work.'"

Mrs. Muldoon went on to recount his last days. She said, "In the end, he rarely left his room and said the rosary alone. One night he went down to the dining room at dinner. I wheeled him into the room and noticed that he was carrying a bottle of wine in his lap. He asked the waitress to pour each priest a glass. Then he proposed a toast. 'To the Pope, bishops and us Priests who were and are in the trenches, Salud.' I guess it was his way of saying goodbye. He died in his sleep about a week later."

When Bishop Hogan returned to his office, he noted the brown envelope on his desk. He pulled each staple apart and opened the envelope. It was hand written on yellow paper with green lines. It read:

Dear Bishop Hogan,

This will get to you after I'm gone. That's the way I want it. This is written with the highest respect for you and your position as Bishop. Ubi Episcopus, ibi Ecclesia. Where the Bishop is, there you will find the Church. I write this letter out of my love for the priesthood and for no other reason.

When your predecessor died a few years ago and you were appointed to this See, I was very happy, even though I had never met you. As usual when there is a transition like that, some priests don't welcome the new Bishop. But you handled it very well and won those priests over. You didn't make any big changes before you got to know the territory. I read your book on the priesthood and liked it very much. Through the grapevine I heard of your work with Priests' support groups and that you belonged to such a group yourself. I think we need that type of assembly here too, not because we have bad Priests here. On the contrary, we have many fine Priests as you've already observed. I think we lack something in our fraternity. That is, showing our love for each other in an atmosphere of prayer. Yes, we have retreats, meetings and other conferences. But we do need support groups. I was hoping that you could push that here. Over a period of time with discussions on a local level we could lay out a plan, which would be strictly voluntary. I ask you to think about it and use your experience from your former diocese.

You know, I was ordained maybe before you were born and go back a long way. In the old days young priests weren't treated so well. I'm glad those times are over. I've told Mrs. Muldoon about my escapades. She could write a book about me. I was already living in this Home when the 'turmoils' occurred. The abused crisis has been a difficult time for us, as we are smeared all over the press and on television. I don't think it's fair to target one group without acknowledging that the problem of abuse is across the board. In the end, in the history of the Church, we always come out purified and renewed. I think this type of interaction could be the beginning of the renewal of the priesthood. Have we learned anything from the 'turmoil'?? I hope so. I say my rosary every day that we will be cleansed, beautified and purified and that we will come out stronger, better and more prayerful. The media has brought us to our knees. Well, that's where we should be.

At these assemblies (I dislike the word 'meeting' in this context), we could read a passage from Scripture and have an open discussion on how these words affect us. We could elect a chairman to keep us on the right track. That would be absolutely necessary. Then we could discuss an article from some catholic magazine or book. We could have an open discussion on various topics. For instance, we could examine the treatment of divorced Catholics, preparation for Confirmation, the Liturgy and so on. We are deeply divided on some issues. We are either far right or far left. We really need a meeting of minds. If we can't have a civil discussion, then where are we? We could have confessions at the end lunch. There a hundred ways we could run the discussions, but as Your Excellency has proved, it's worth an effort. Please pray to St. Joseph for me that I will have a happy death and be forgiven my sins. Oremus pro invicem.

In Jesus, the great High Priest,

Milky

Bishop Hogan opened support groups throughout his Diocese. They were well received and continue to thrive. The Pope Himself heard about Bishop Hogan's desire to unite his priests through support groups. His Holiness suggested that he write a book about the renewal of the priesthood. It took two years to finish the book and edit it. It is called "The Priesthood We Share." It was dedicated to Fr. J"M"H. The M was in quotation marks.

The Disappearance of Fr. Mario Bernardino

Mother Clare died in her sleep at the Poor Clare's Convent in Baltimore, Maryland. She had been a police detective in Philadelphia. After twenty years of police work, Mary Collins retired and with the counseling of her uncle, Bishop Jeffrey Collins (later Archbishop and Cardinal in St. Louis), she entered the convent here. She was forty-two at the time. When we went through her belongings, we found a report she filed when she was a detective. Mother Mary Theresa, her successor, read the report with great interest. I , Sr. Jude, was the first Counselor, and was given the file to read. It was a copy that she had sent to Cardinal Fahey of Philadelphia. It deals with the disappearance of Fr. Mario Bernardino. Mary Collins was given the assignment from the Police commissioner of finding Fr. Mario. Mary (Mother Clare) was on the force twelve years, when she was given this duty. The following is a copy of Mary's remembrance of the task.

All that is written here has already been filed properly with the appropriate authorities, both in the Church and in the police archives. I want to put down in order my recollections of this strange case.

I was the detective on duty that bitterly cold night in February, when I received a phone call from the Commissioner who told me that one of the Archdiocesan priests was reported missing by Cardinal Fahey, and he asked for me to look into the case. He suggested I meet with the Cardinal as soon as possible. Evidently the priest was in very good standing, and had vanished into thin air on his day off. His car was found vandalized near the race track in New Jersey, but there was no trace whatsoever of Fr. Bernardino. I called Cardinal Fahey immediately, even though it was two o'clock in the morning. The Cardinal related that Fr. Bernardino was a popular priest and that there were no rumors of anything dark in his personality. Fr. Bernardino, he explained, came from a devout Catholic family from South Philadelphia. He was a family man, who visited his mother and sister Gloria almost every Sunday evening. Gloria was a Summa Cum Laude graduate of the University of Pennsylvania and was a Vice-President of a large Insurance Company. She had a salary of six figures. The clan respected Mama Bernardino and delighted in her delicious pasta, of which she was an expert. His father and mother were immigrants. His dad was an outstanding stone fitter, and had done well in his business. His mother had been brought over from the Abruzzi as a bride. She could play the piano and taught the clan many songs, which they sang frequently. Mario was the apple of his parents' eyes, but when he decided to enter the seminary, they encouraged him.

Father Bernardino entered St. Charles Seminary in Overbrook, Pennsylvania after graduating from a Catholic High School. After Ordination to the Priesthood, he was assigned to parishes around the Archdiocese. The Cardinal called in Fr. Mario and asked him to attend Villanova University to get a degree in Science so that he could teach high school. At Villanova, Mario did extremely well in his studies and earned a Master's Degree in Science along with credits in Education that were required by the State. Mario minored in Astronomy under the legendary scholar Fr. Philip "Phil" Janis, who was an expert in the study of the heavens. Mario and Phil became close friends and used to study the stars on a telescope in the University's laboratory. They enjoyed going to an Irish Pub together near the University, even though Phil was a Polish American and Mario was an Italian American.

We interviewed Fr. Janis who was well known for his quiet good humor and his passion for Astronomy. "Yes," he said, "I knew Mario very well. You know he had the potential to be a good scientist. I recommended to the Cardinal that he be sent to MIT or Stanford to get a Doctorate. The Cardinal, however, had a "slot" in mind at a high school where he wanted Mario to go." Fr. Janis went on to say that Mario had been one of his best students and that they had remained good friends. I asked Fr. Janis if there was anything he could think of that might give a clue to Fr. Bernardino's disappearance. Fr. Janis flushed a little and said, "well, there was one thing that Mario was unscientific about. That was his belief in UFOs and the tiny people who inhabit the universe. On this, Mario was quite daffy. He said he had an intuition that they would contact him some day. Did you know he was called on the carpet in the Diocesan Educational Office and told to desist from telling his students that he believed in UFOs? I kidded him about it, but it didn't hurt our friendship."

It's interesting that Fr. Bernardino taught me in high school and had lived for a time in my parish. Some of the girls had a "crush" on him. One of the students was watching Turner's Classic Movies with her grandmother and saw Rudolf Valentino on the screen. She told us about him, and how Fr. Bernardino resembled him. We all thought he was "cute" and nicknamed him "Rudi." Father was a very good, clear teacher and a fair marker. He was unflappable and rarely showed anger. He disliked it very much, when a student talked in class. He would put his hands on his hips, glare at the student and say, "I'm waiting. I'm waiting." He helped students, who were weak in their studies, after class. Our school had a reputation for doing well in Mathematics and Science.

In our investigation we found not only that Fr. Bernardino believed in UFOs. He also had another hobby, the ponies. This seemed to be his favorite pastime. Actually, we found that he bet very little. It was the atmosphere and excitement that he enjoyed. He disappeared near the race track in New Jersey.

My investigation naturally took me to the rectory, where Fr. Bernardino was living at the time when he vanished from sight. Fr. Edward "Ned" Sullivan was pastor and Thomas "Tom" Weiseman was associate pastor. Although we had searched his room for clues before, we decided to look again with the knowledge we had gained up to this point in our investigation. We were looking for clues that might lead us to some reason for his disappearance. We had asked the pastor not to touch anything in the room, and found that the bed was made, indicating that he had not slept that night. The room was very orderly, with a telescope near the window. There were some books in his bookcase and some Catholic magazines on his desk. One of the magazines was "The Wanderer" (a right wing newspaper) and "The Pope Speaks" (a traditional review of the Pope's speeches and sermons). There was a diary in his desk drawer, which must have been overlooked in the first search. Since I didn't think it was appropriate to read the journal before showing it to the Cardinal, I put it into my brief case. I handed it over to the Cardinal with the intention of giving it to the Commissioner. I was allowed to see the diary at a later date. Neither the Cardinal nor the Commissioner made any comments. Actually, it was his teaching schedule in high school and not a diary in the strict sense, even though he had written the dates on some observations he had made. There was a name card in the diary, with the name John Bennet on it. The card said that Mr. Bennet was the author of a book on UFO's. I noticed that his phone number was listed, and I was determined to call him as soon as possible.

In my interview with the two priests who were stationed there, I found out immediately that Fr. Sullivan and Fr. Bernardino had not been on good terms. Evidently Fr. Sullivan thought that Fr. Bernardino's views on the existence of UFOs were unorthodox and indeed heretical. Fr. Sullivan admitted that they had heated arguments on this subject. Father Bernardino always held his own in this theological argument. He contended that this was an open question, and that the magisterium had made no comments on the issue. Fr. Sullivan's ideas were twofold. First, if there actually were people living in outer space, how are they affected by original sin, and secondly how are they saved under the blood of Christ? Fr. Bernardino could only conjecture on these points. Actually, these questions were "gotcha" ways of argument. Fr. Bernardino was absolutely convinced of the existence of space people, and that they were interested in our planet. These quarrels evidently were frequent in the rectory, especially over martinis.

Fr. Weiseman was terrified of Fr. Sullivan, but he and Fr. Bernardino got on well. "He rarely mentioned his ideas on UFOs to me. He was very nice and considerate. He never spoke ill of Fr. Sullivan or anyone for that matter. He wanted me to become a high school teacher like himself, but I'm not interested in going down that road unless forced to do so by the Cardinal. I'd be very reluctant," he said with simplicity.

The live-in house keeper came from the neighborhood, said she thought Fr. Bernardino was a very nice man. He had taught her to make authentic Italian spaghetti which she prepared once a week without fail. "No," she said, "He never spoke to me about UFOs, but he used to watch the stars with his telescope. He made no secret about the fact that he went to the race track. People used to joke with him about that. I think he had a bookie, because he told me not to transfer calls to him after ten thirty PM. He would take all calls directly. Once, when he was away, I answered the phone late at night and a male voice said, 'this is the midget.' When I asked who? The connection was promptly broken. When I relayed this strange message to Fr. Bernardino, he said, 'shhhhhhh.' Fr. Sullivan was very jealous of him because of his popularity. Priests are like that, you know. I can read priests like a book. They're very jealous people."

Another detective and I checked out the vandalized car, which was in the police compound. It had been stripped clean, and there was no evidence that could help in our investigation. Things were becoming to look a little creepy.

It was time to have an interview with Fr. Bernardino's family. It goes without saying that his mother and sister were devastated by the vanishing of Mario. His mother, Mama Bernardino, and his sister, Gloria, were anxious to talk about this bazaar event. "He was a good priest. We can't imagine what happened to him. His only interests were teaching science and going to the race track," his mother said with tears in her eyes. Gloria had her brother's financial accounts in a brown envelope. He received about twenty thousand dollars a year for teaching and another five thousand dollars from Mass stipends. He had about thirteen thousand in safe CDs. He didn't like to speculate. The diocesan policy was that you had to enter room and board as income and pay taxes on them. This came to about thirty five thousand a year. He had about three thousand in his checking account to cover his checks and credit cards." I asked them about UFOs, and they answered that he thought that aliens existed, but so do many people. We didn't think that was strange. It was never a topic of conversation. "Anything else?" I asked. "Well," answered Mama Bernardino, "He had a bookie named the Midget, who called here once or twice late at night. We asked about this fellow, and he just laughed and changed the subject. We would love to know who this bookie is. We admonished him not to play the numbers, because it can get addictive." "Well," I said, "that creepy name has popped up before. We'll have to use informants to find out who he is." "Do you think he's dead?" Gloria asked with grave concern. "We'll consider him alive," I said, "until we have definite proof that he is dead. In my gut, I have to say that I think he's alive somewhere. We'll put a priority on finding him."

My assistant, Detective Ferguson, and I visited Father Bernardino's poker playing priest friends. They were all of Irish descent. They admitted that Mario was a very conservative poker player, and was happy if he broke even. "Patience is the art of poker," he would say. They laughed, and said that sometimes he pulled off outrageous bluffs. He often won on that, and would say, "man, I love to beat you Micks." They all concurred that Mario was a lot of fun. "UFOs?" I asked, and they shook their heads as if they were baffled. "Yes, he believed in them. We joked about his ideas with him, but on this point he was dead serious. But so what" they answered. I could tell they wanted to get back to playing cards.

A week or so had gone by since Father Bernardino vanished. The Cardinal called me and asked if I had checked out any "snitches." The press was very keen on Father Bernardino's whereabouts and published stories almost every day. Their journalists were searching too. Our informants had no idea who the Midget was, but they were adamant that it was not a bookie in this city. They were very knowledgeable of Father Bernardino's betting, not so much on the numbers but on the ponies. They contended that he only placed bets once or twice a year. We got nowhere there.

We called Mr. Bennet, who lived in Connecticut. He seemed like a pleasant man, and said he would be glad to speak with us. We drove up and he met us at the door of his house and invited us in. His wife was away. We said that a priest in Philadelphia had disappeared, and that we had found Mr. Bennet's name card. "Yes, I know him, but not well. When I had a ceremonial signing of my book, he was there in his roman collar. He was a true believer like me. So we hit it off well. Did you know my book on UFOs sold fifty thousand copies? Fr.Bernardino told me about a secret base in Nevada, where they had a space ship and were designing one for our country. I had heard of that. Actually, there is a base in the Nevada desert, but I don't know if they really have a space ship there. I'm a practicing Catholic myself, and I often use the words about faith in regard to this topic, 'for those who believe, no explanation is necessary, but for those who do not believe no explanation is possible'. Father Bernardino thought that the space people, you know, aliens were going to contact him. He was way out on this point, but that is what he believed." I told him I was very uncomfortable with the idea that belief in UFOs was like an act of faith. He backed down a little, and said that was only an example. I paused a long time and then asked if the term "Midget" was a term used among true believers. He laughed for a long time, and said anyone who has encountered these aliens say that they are very small in stature. Perhaps that's why someone might call them Midgets," and laughed again. "Midgets, that's a good one. That's a good one."

We spent a year on this case and never came up with any answers. Who was the Midget? Could it be that Father Bernardino had been abducted by aliens? Were there other explanations for his disappearance? Do UFOs really exist? Are these aliens watching us? What about that base in Nevada? We will never know the answers. I pray that Fr. Mario is alive and well. He was a good priest, and where ever he is, he's in God's hands.

Signed: Mother Clare Detective Mary Collins

Mother Mary Theresa

Sister Jude

Father John's Miracle

When I look at that old album, prepared and preserved by my mother, it's hard for me to realize that all those snap shots of a lonely looking little boy with no hair and with a complexion as white as the sheets on my hospital bed, is me. Since I was very young, five years old, the memory of my sickness is vague. The events related here are my memories along with those of my mother, which she repeated to me many times over the years. There are also clippings from the newspaper and documents from the doctors and nurses who took care of me.

The family evidently was in a countdown for my death. They thought it might be days or even hours before the Lord would take me. Members of my family were bracing themselves for this eventuality. I was dying of leukemia.

Let me tell you the story in a sequence of events. I recall that a religious sister entered my hospital room, picked me up out of the bed and hugged me tightly. I can recall the scent of flowers. The Nun said to me something like, "John-John (that was my nickname), when you awake, you will be well." I recall a warm feeling, not like the fiery heat of a fever, but like a lukewarm bath that I used to take in my tub before I got sick. When I awoke, there were doctors, nurses and members of my family standing around my bed. My mother relates that a doctor said, "John-John, you're getting better," and I answered, "John-John hungry, John-John hungry." A nurse gave me some ice cream which I devoured and asked for more. "John-John thirsty," I said and began to drink fruit juices. The doctor said, "He has no fever, his blood pressure is normal and there is no unnecessary fluid in his lungs. He is in remission." "My God, it's like a miracle," one of the nurses said. "Nice lady hug John-John," I said in a strong voice. "What lady, John-John?" my mother asked, "There is no lady." "Nice lady hold John-John. John-John smell flowers," I persisted. Then the supervisor of the hospital, a Nun, reached under my pillow and showed me a picture, a holy card, of their founder with the face of Jeanne Marie Cross on it. "Is this the lady who hugged you, John-John?" she asked. "Yes," I answered. "That's the nice lady who holds John-John." The superior of the convent of Sisters who ran the hospital turned to my mother and said, "We put a relic of Mother Cross under John-John's pillow and at night prayer, we begged the Lord that through the intercession of our founder John-John would have a complete recovery. This seems to be a miracle." Indeed it was. All traces of my cancer were gone. My mom, dad, and my elder sisters all hugged me. They were all crying with joy.

After that I had to remain in the hospital for tests to confirm that I had fully recovered. I also had x-rays to document this miracle by comparing the old x-rays with the new ones. The Mother Superior wanted scientific evidence of my healing. She interviewed the doctors and nurses who had attended me for their written statements, and on tape recordings. The nurse, a non-Catholic, who was on duty that night, related to us how she had gone out of my room for a few seconds to get some towels. She said my breathing was very heavy, that I was unconscious, and had a very high fever. When she returned to my room, she said that I was sleeping peacefully without a temperature. She rang an urgency bell for a doctor to come. She also called the Supervisor. The Mother Superior documented all these things and intended to present them to Rome for the canonization of Mother Cross. After a few years of waiting, we heard that Rome had approved the miracle.

Many years later, when I was a Jesuit seminarian studying for the Priesthood, the Order of Nuns who administered that hospital asked me to come to Rome to attend the Canonization of Mother Cross. My miracle was the third one attributed to Mother Cross and like mine was highly documented. Even though the language of the Mass was in French, I was honored to do the first reading in English. In a private meeting with the Holy Father, the Mother Superior introduced me as "one of the cures." The Holy Father told me that my miracle wasn't accidental, and that I should dedicate my life to being a good priest and to spread this work of God.

I joined the Jesuits after graduating from St. Louis University. I had also graduated from a Jesuit High School. It's my greatest honor to be a member of the Society of Jesus. I was given every opportunity to prepare myself academically for a life of ministry in the Church. Our formation takes many years. We even make a second Novitiate, usually in a foreign country, to prepare for Ordination. I look back infrequently on my long formation process. I'll tell you one story. When I was a Novice we had to speak to each other in Latin. The first words I memorized, as suggested by upper classmen, were "carnem si vis, and panem si vis" (please pass the meat and please pass the bread). Those words served me well.

After gaining a Masters Degree in English from Fordham University in New York, I was sent to Oxford to work for a higher degree in English Literature. The traditions and formality at Oxford were very pleasing to me. I spent three years pursuing my degree. I was lucky enough to do sightseeing in merry England, green Ireland and lovely Scotland. My family, when they visited me, said I had become an English gentleman. When I was finishing my thesis on Coleridge, our Father General visited with me in London. He said he wanted me to go the Jesuit University, Sophia, in

Tokyo to build up their English Department. When I arrived in Tokyo I was sent to our advanced Language School in Kamakura, near Yokohama. It was quite rigorous study for me, more difficult than anything I had studied before. The Jesuits who had done their Theology in Japan were already fluent in speaking and quite competent in the Japanese written language. I've spent my life here teaching English, first in High School in Hiroshima and then at Sophia University in Tokyo where I also participated in administration. I was Dean for a few years at our International School attached to Sophia, in which the language is English. There were many foreigners from around the globe and many Japanese who had studied abroad, and even though they could speak Japanese, they were not capable in the written language to compete for the entrance examinations to prestigious Universities.

Sophia University in Tokyo is situated in Yottsuya, one of the busiest, upscale parts of Tokyo. It is highly rated thanks to the vision of early missionaries from Germany, Italy, Spain and the United States. Our English and Foreign Service Departments are considered to be among the best in Japan. Many of the students are graduates of Catholic High Schools. In Japan high schools are rated by the number of students who advance to prestigious Universities. We have never had trouble enrolling students.

I taught English Literature in the University for many years. The students had to handle Shakespeare, poets, essayists, novelists and other famous authors. The English entrance exam was so difficult that even I didn't know some of the answers. In prominent high schools, the students have to read Time Magazine in preparation for our entrance exam. I got to know many of the students, some of whom became Catholics in later life. The Japanese Bishops permit non-Christians to be married in church. Often I would have two marriage ceremonies on the same day. We kept contact over the years. Both the male and female students did extremely well in society. The graduates often married one another. When there were fixed marriages, our women graduates were often chosen to be a bride, because of the background of having graduated from Sophia. I often took lunch in the dining room where the servers knew I liked noodles. There was a special room for the professors, and we often had chats together and formed friendships. I avoided academic politics like the plague, knowing that anything I said would be repeated. Academics, you know, thrive on politics. In the students' dining room my pupils often ate with me. We loved to kid each other. They called me "Yohane sensei" (teacher John) or "yohane Shimpusan" (Father John). I ran a Bible study class in English, which was quite popular. From those classes some students were later baptized.

I also ran evening adult study groups in the Bible, both in English and Japanese. I got to know many people in various life styles and in the work place. I always told them about my healing, when I was a child. With pictures of me before and after my cure, I related the story. But they believed that there must be some scientific, medical reason for my recovery, and said they found it hard to believe in miracles.

I have to tell you about a middle age woman named Akabane, who talked to me after class about my sickness and rehabilitation. She was married to a famous doctor from Keio University, who was interested in my tale and wanted to meet me. She invited me over to her house and we had a delicious steak dinner. She thought, as many Japanese think, that foreigners cannot adjust to typical native cuisine. We had a long discussion of my case. I showed them the pictures of me in the hospital and some clippings I had preserved. The doctor was very adamant at first that there had to be a rational, scientific reason for my case. Both the husband and the wife were highly cultured, and in an indirect Japanese way they indicated in a polite way that there must be a reason for such a cure. I just left it at that. It was a natural conclusion for them. One thing, though, we became very close friends. We met about every three months or so for sushi or other types of Japanese cuisine. We had a joke between us. At the dinner, Mrs. Akabane would say, "my, your good with chopsticks," (Japanese think that a foreigner could never adapt to their use). I would answer, " thank you for the compliment, but my mother was Chinese." At that they both would bow and say, "hooooooooo," (a Japanese expression for being truly amazed). Mrs. Akabane was an expert on Japanese polite language. Her husband would tease her by using high class feminine language in a high voice.

Doctor Akabane who was the chairman of his department at the hospital asked me to speak to his staff and some patients. I told them that health care was not just a job. It was a call to love. I then read from St. Paul's letter to the Corinthians the famous words, "love is kind," etc. I took each expression on love and explained it with examples from hospital life. This was extremely well received. At the end of my talk, a nurse asked me to read the passage again, which I did. They all applauded. Through Dr. Akabane's influence, I was asked to speak at other hospitals in the Tokyo area. Surprisingly, many people I met at these hospitals were knowledgeable of the Bible, either by attempting to read it themselves or by studying at Christian schools. They were admirers of Jesus from a distance, especially for his non-judgmental attitude toward those who were ritually unclean. The graduates of Protestant Universities related how they had morning prayers with hymns in the chapel every morning. A passage from the Bible was read and one of the Protestant teachers would give an explanation. Evidently, they complained about this practice while they were students. However in later years, they looked back with nostalgia on their student days. There are many graduates of these famous protestant schools who are prominent writers, musicians, architects, politicians, leaders on the political scene and CEO's of large corporations.

Our Jesuit approach to education is different from other Christian schools, even though we have the same aim. In our high schools, we provide Bible study both for the students and the parents on a voluntary basis. Surprisingly, when you think of the teen age years, many students persevered in learning catechism and the Bible. The mothers also studied the bible with us. As in other Christian schools, we had a strong Fathers' Club, which was very supportive of our plans. So there is a great Jesuit influence in our schools. We try to nurture Jesuit values in our teachers and staff. I've been caught up in this mission and have enjoyed every minute of it.

I retired from teaching three years ago. I thought they would give me a rocking chair and a pipe to smoke, so that I could relax and enjoy the golden years. Well, I've entered a new apostolate of preaching retreats, mostly to students and the staff in Catholic schools. I've also been directing priests' retreats and have gotten good feedback from this ministry. Last year, I was asked if I would like to do parish work, but I declined. Recently, I was asked to be on the formation team. I'll probably hear from my Superiors one of these days.

I would like tell you of an interesting event that happened to one of our Sophia graduates about two years ago. This fellow, whom I knew very well, was motor cycling in the beautiful hot spring resort in Nikko, not far from Tokyo. He had an accident and was severely injured. He was flown by helicopter to Keio University hospital. When I heard this sad news, I rushed over to the hospital to comfort the family and to pray for the man. Without revealing it to the parents, I placed a relic and picture of Mother Cross under the patient's pillow. In the corner of the room, I said the Catholic prayers for the dying. He seemed to be completely paralyzed, was unconscious, and breathing very heavily. After praying by myself for a short time, I left the hospital and returned to our house in Yottsuya. I went directly to the chapel and continued my prayers begging for the life of my former pupil. No one thought that he would make it. The next morning I said Mass for the man (he was no longer a boy). I continued my prayers for a few days. Then I received a phone call from the mother, who told me with great joy that her son had taken a turn for the better and that his doctors said that he had passed the crisis. He was alert, drinking tea and eating custard. "Kiseki, Kiseki," (miracle, miracle) his mother repeated. I rushed over to the hospital and was greeted with great joy by the family. They said it was my prayers that saved their son. "We smelt flowers right before he awoke. It must have been God." Since they were non-Christians, I told them that I too thought it was a miracle. I thought it was too complicated to tell them about Mother Cross. But I knew. The aroma of flowers at the time of the man's turning point was proof to me that God had acted through the intercession of Mother Cross.

Dr. Akabane was aware of this case. When we spoke together, he said that he heard that I was there and that I had prayed for the injured man. "When I heard that there was a scent of flowers, I remembered the story of your cure. I'm a skeptical guy and don't believe anything that can't be proved outside the microscope. Maybe God does work in mysterious ways that we cannot fathom." Mrs. Akabane was convinced it was a miracle. She was baptized into the Catholic Church last Holy Saturday night. Her husband was there at the ceremony. "Maybe someday he will find God," his wife said. "I'm sure he will. He is such a sincere man. The miracle he had seen before his eyes made him consider the existence of God."

So it seems with that miracle, my life has come full circle. Through the intercession of Mother Cross, I was not only healed physically but also through her, God had led me my whole life. I remember what the Holy Father told me at Mother Cross' canonization, that my cure wasn't accidental. It was meant for me to be a worthy priest and spread the Good News of Jesus Christ. The other night Joe Rogers from Philly came to my room. He made a gesture with his nose as if he was smelling something. "Hey, man, you use too much deodorant. It smells like flowers in here."

Father Dave's Redemption

Father Dave Norris, a Naval Chaplain during the Vietnam War, left the military in good standing. He had a long career, had the respect of his superiors (mostly Protestant Chaplains), and was well liked by the seamen in his charge. Fr. Dave had distinguished himself under fire during the retreat from Danang. He was ordered back to the base by the Marine Captain in charge. He was never cited for gallantry, but when he met the Captain again, the Captain said, "Ya done good, Father, ya done good. You're not like that wishy-washy Reverend on M.A.S.H. I can't stand that guy."

In the next few days, Fr. Dave visited the camp hospital many times, and got to know the superb doctors and nurses serving there. He noticed an Asian looking nurse, who approached him and said that her name was Maria Kim, a Korean American from Seattle. Her parents were wed in the old country, but had immigrated to America during the war in Vietnam. At the Officers' dining room he met First Lieutenant Kim again, and she came over to his table carrying a slice of pizza and a beer. "I'd like to go to confession some time, Father," she said and sat down. "Sure, any time. I'm always available," the priest answered. The confidence that Catholics placed in the priest was a source of joy to Dave, even though he knew perfectly well that his lack of faith was not the appropriate way to administer the Sacraments of the Church.

Fr. Dave knew he should never have joined the military. On the outside, he was a good Chaplain and a fine Officer. On the inside, he felt empty. He only said scheduled Mass for the troops when he had to. He had given up completely on his Breviary, his rosary and any other kind of prayer. Prayer didn't fit into his busy schedule. He became just like any other officer in seeking rank. On this point he was quite ambitious. He smoked cigars, drank beer in the Marine Officers' dining room, and was noted for being tight lipped. Never once was he cited for inappropriate behavior. He was hurt to the core when a high ranking marine said to him with some sarcasm, "What are you a Chaplain, or just a career officer?" "I'm both, sir, and proud of it," Father Dave answered, but both parties knew that Dave was faking it. When he told that story to a friend in the dining room, the friend said, "That guy is rarely wrong in his assessment of character."

49

When he was preparing for Mass, he noticed a black Officer sitting in the back of the auditorium. They stared at each other, and both noticed at the same time that they knew each other from high school in Washington, where Dave had been an English teacher for six years. They approached each other and shook hands. "Brutus was an honorable man," he said, referring to Shakespeare's Julius Caesar that he had studied under Dave a few years before. Dave recalled the student, Cliff Gilbert, who had been a wide receiver on the football team at the school in Washington. "How are you, Cliff?" Dave said as they shook hands. "Hey, it's good to see you, Father," the young officer responded. "You were a great football player, Cliff. I remember you caught two touchdowns in one game. We thought you might get a scholarship," Dave continued with admiration. "Yeah, the scouts checked me out, but who would want a hundred and forty pound player? Joe Paterno met me and said to come back, if I gained a few pounds. I got some offers from some small colleges, but I was interested in going to Annapolis and was selected with the help of a politician, who was a graduate of our school. And here I am." They went over to the Officers' Club and had some coffee. "One thing I can remember from those days, Father, was that we used to serve Mass for the priests and afterwards, we were given coffee and doughnuts. I don't remember seeing you, Father," Cliff mentioned in passing. "Yeah, well, I used to have the Nuns' convents," Dave lied. Cliff was killed in action a few weeks later.

After Cliff left, Dave reminisced of his younger days in the seminary and his first assignment at the high school in Washington. Dave was a skillful teacher but was not much for community life. He hardly ever went to prayers, and only said Mass when he was sent to a parish on Sundays. He really wanted to get out of teaching. He would prefer parish life or becoming a chaplain in the armed service. When Dave talked to the Father Provincial, he mentioned his desire for a change and of his aspiration to become a chaplain. The Provincial was very hesitant, because of Dave's track record in his first assignment. "Yeah, well, why don't we think this out? A chaplain is a special vocation. Why don't we think about it for a year or so? I have to say, Dave, that you're teaching is excellent and the kids like you, but after that you seem to use the Monastery as a hotel. I hear you don't participate in anything. But if you shape up in a year, I'll give it another review." Dave returned to the high school and did his best to attend prayers and say Mass. After a year, he approached the Provincial again. "Well, Dave, I have real concerns but after my Council advised me that I should give you a chance, I reluctantly agreed. I'll tell you frankly, Dave, that if you don't have a spiritual basis, you will not make it as a chaplain or anything else for that matter," the Provincial counseled him in a very sober way. After his training, Dave became a chaplain in the Marines. He was sent to various bases in the United States before receiving his orders for Vietnam. The vacuum in his heart continued there. He kept remembering the Provincial's advice. His adverse feelings of the way the top military officers were running the war also affected his life as a priest. His dejection was heightened, when he saw the body bags and severely wounded Marines. Just before the fall of Saigon, Dave was sent back to America. He then decided to leave the military. The meaningless war and his own spiritual desolation were distinct signs that he should return to his Province.

Dave was sent to one of his Order's parishes in upstate New York. He loved the people, and his pastor was a fine gentleman who complimented Dave on various occasions. In his sermons, he used his experience in the Marines to give examples. He visited hospitals, said Mass in homes for the elderly, prepared the children for Confirmation and ran a Bible class. After a couple of years, Dave decided to leave his Order and the Priesthood. He could use his pension from the Navy and maybe find another job. He requested a meeting with his Provincial who had been reelected. The Provincial was deeply saddened by Dave's decision. He cautioned Dave not to rush into such a turn in his life. He mentioned to Dave about a counselor they used in the Province. "Her name is Sister Ann Tyler. She's a practicing psychologist with a lot of experience in helping religious and priests. She's a great listener and has a lot of wisdom. Why don't you talk to her, Dave?" the Provincial said in a very serious voice.

Sr. Ann turned out to be a compassionate and insightful counselor. In three interviews, she only asked Dave questions and then noted his answers in her notebook. Dave told her of his happy childhood, his seminary life, priestly years, and military life. He told her how he came to despise the war. He said he had no resentment whatsoever with his Order nor the priesthood itself. He had no desire at that time to marry and emphasized that this was not why he wanted to leave. He told her of the state of his soul and how he had gradually given up on prayer. "My problems are spiritual," he said. "I think I lost my faith. I don't know why. I hope you won't be shocked, when I say that any more, I just don't give a damn. Maybe I'll find myself outside the priesthood. It would be hypocritical to continue in this state of mind." Sr. Ann stared at Dave for a long time and then commented, "You're so honest, Father. You pinpointed your problem as lack of faith. I'm a little surprised at that. Most of my cases deal with deep seated resentment or a desire to marry but they usually don't identify their problems as coming from lack of faith. She paused a long time and then suggested, "why don't you take some time off and think about your decision? Frankly, I'm worried about your spiritual life. Don't you see that the devil can crush you like grapes in a Spanish vat? You're almost on the verge of despair. If you don't confront this problem of faith you could jeopardize your eternal salvation." Sr. Ann urged Dave to go to a Trappist Monastery in the south for a period of discernment. Dave, after speaking with his Father Provincial, decided to take Sr. Ann's advice. In her report to the Provincial, she said that at this stage in Dave's life, she would counsel that he had to find himself spiritually. She continued that she wasn't advising therapy and/or medication. "That will come later if he needs it. Oh, he's such an honest priest. I think he'll make it."

Dave put his bags in the hallway of the visitors' house not far from the Abbey. A middle aged Brother welcomed Dave and showed him his room, which was well furnished with his own bathroom and shower. "Hey, Father, I'm Brother Julian. I'm responsible for the visitors' house. Anything you need, just call on me," the Brother said in a cheerful voice. "You might want to check in with the Abbot over in the Monastery. You'll like him. He's a great guy."

The Abbot met Dave, and he seemed very warm and pleasant. "Welcome, Father. I hope you have a profitable time here. Come and go as you like. There's a big mall down the road. Many visitors come frequently. You can mingle with them. Sometimes Priests come for retreat," he said with great cordiality. "Yes," answered Dave. "I guess you read a report about me. I have problems of faith. It's partly my fault, as I gave up on all the spiritual exercises I learned in the Novitiate. It was a gradual thing. I thought the military would give me a new view point, but things got worse. I'm in a real pickle now. I'm honest enough to know that I'm a hypocrite. I don't think that it's right to continue as a priest if you don't believe and God is not in your life," Dave said as he bared his soul. "Actually, I did get reports from both your Provincial and Sr. Ann," the Abbot responded. "They both said you were very honest and if you find yourself, you can return to ministry." Dave looked down and said, "Whether I quit the Priesthood or not, I can't live without God. I was so intent when I was young." Dave left the Abbot's room and returned to the visitors' house. He missed dinner because he slept right up until 10 PM. He hadn't noticed how exhausted he was. He continued to sleep late and take long naps in the afternoon.

For a couple of weeks Dave made friends with the visitors who came and went. He met some priests who were there making private retreats. One priest told him he had left the priesthood but never married. He was admitted back into the clergy and, he said he had a happy life. Not knowing of Dave's state of mind, he said, "Say your prayers, man. That's where it's at." Dave went frequently to the Mall, walked around and usually had Mexican food. He bought odds and ends for his room and some shirts that he didn't need. He always spent some time in the book store and glanced at the new best sellers. Finally, he would go over to the soda fountain and have a milk shake, which he liked very much. In the evenings, he watched TV, while continuously surfing the channels. He read briefly before sleeping. Never in his life had he suffered from insomnia. He slept the whole night.

He met Brother Julian often, and they chatted a little bit. On his walks around the grounds, he observed the priests and brothers doing chores. They cut down trees, mowed the lawns, took care of the farm and some animals, and made ceramics and wood carvings, which they sold to the visitors. At Christmas, they made and shipped fruit cakes. They were able to sustain themselves by their own work. Dave could hear them chanting, when he walked past their chapel. He went in one time and sat in the back. He recognized the Divine Office, which he had chanted when he was a seminarian. The piety and sense of prayer of the community impressed Dave very much.

One day Brother Julian invited him to go to the book store, which was usually filled with visitors. The Brothers did very artistic work. As Dave checked out the statues and rosaries, he noticed that Brother Julian was searching for a book. He then came over to Dave and offered him a volume of the autobiography of St. Theresa, known as the Little Flower. Dave knew of the book well, but had never read it. "Take it on me, Father. I'll confess it at our chapter of faults. They all will boo me," he said and then chuckled. Dave took the book to his room and placed it in the book case. It lay there for a week or so, until Dave picked it up and glanced through it. He observed immediately that the Little Flower spoke frequently about her temptations against faith. Dave read the book over a period of a week and then read it again. This young Nun's explanation of the temptations to the spiritual life was so near to Dave's state of mind that he felt that it was uncanny. He met Brother Julian in the garden and told him how much he enjoyed the book. "She's just like me," Dave said. Julian answered, "Yeah, she's just like all of us." He then went over to a rose bush, cut off a branch, gave it to Dave and said, "this rose is from St. Theresa. She sent me one a long time ago."

The rest is history, as they say. Dave went to confession to the Abbot and started participating in the Divine Office and Mass. The Abbot urged him to concelebrate. At the prayer of the Faithful, Dave said, "Through the intercession of St. Theresa, may all troubled priests find their way back to God." At the sign of peace the priests and Brothers came one by one and embraced him. The Abbot called Dave aside after Mass, and requested him to be the main celebrant the following day. At the Mass, Dave related his conversion through the grace of God with the help of the Little Flower. After the Mass, Dave got his bags packed and returned to his Province. He met the Father Provincial and Sr. Ann. "We knew you'd make it, Father. You're so honest," Sister said. Dave was given a new assignment in parish work. He loves to use his Marine Corps terms "Chow, saddle up, semper fi, and stand down." He was often asked to give priests' retreats. His background was the chief source of his stories. He kept repeating, "don't give up on your prayer life. It's your only salvation." Many priests came to him for confession. He was indeed pleased, that he could help other priests who were troubled.

SPEEDY GONZALES, FR. NICK LACETO

Young Frank Donovan

The Makings of a Cardinal

On May 6, 1989 Jeffrey Cardinal Collins, retired Prelate of St. Louis, had kind of a bazaar death. He liked to drive over to the nearby parish church to go to confession. Even though he wasn't feeling well that night, he decided to receive the Sacrament of Reconciliation anyway. It was about 8:30 PM. After confession, he knelt in a pew on the far left side of the church, and said his penance and daily rosary. He began to feel nauseous, and burped up some up some of his dinner on to his clerical shirt. Then he fainted, and slid under the bench, where he was not visible to anyone. A few minutes after nine, the sacristan came into the church to close the doors. Cardinal Collins, conscious or unconscious, we do not know, went unnoticed. The next morning a religious sister, spiritual director of the parish, walked down the aisle and noticed a rosary on the bench. When she went to retrieve it, she noticed that someone was lying under the pew. She went into the sacristy and called the young priest who was preparing for Mass. The priest asked the sacristan to accompany him. When the three of them pulled the bench back, they recognized the Cardinal. Sister went over and touched his neck for a pulse, "He's still alive, but has a weak pulse. Father, get the Sacred Oils to anoint him." When the priest entered the sacristy, he immediately called 911 and told them it was an emergency. He ran back to the place where Cardinal Collins was lying. He whispered into the Cardinal's ear, "Your Excellency, if you can hear me, make an act of contrition. I'm going to give you the Sacrament of the Sick." Minutes later, the paramedics arrived. The technician tried to find a pulse, but Cardinal Collins was dead.

The wake and funeral were carried out with great respect and dignity. During the wake thousands of people passed the coffin, and many were weeping. The ceremony of the Mass was handled by Bishop Thomas Hogan, a close friend of the Cardinal, who emphasized in his homily that Cardinal Collins was above all a man of intense faith, which was shown in his life of prayer and his dedication to the Blessed Mother. Bishop Hogan spoke of his long friendship with the Cardinal and praised his long service to the Church, especially to Catholic Education and welfare for the poor.

Mary Jo Flanigan, Cardinal Collins' grandniece, who was an author and playwright, attended the funeral Mass. Although she had met the Cardinal as a little girl, she only knew what the extended family said about him. She was intrigued by the life and background of the Cardinal. She decided to do research on the

Cardinal's life and write a book about her granduncle. She thought it might be interesting to Catholic readers, and beyond how a boy just out of high school could go all the way to the Red Hat. Rather than focus on the many controversies that the Cardinal had faced in his ministry, Mary Jo wanted to show what his early life was like, his seminary days, life as a priest, a Bishop and then a Cardinal.

She started research on the book by first interviewing some of the members of the family, who knew Jeffry from his youth and were very close to him. Evidently, he was a great competitor in sports from his early childhood. He wanted to beat his elder brothers in any and every sport available. His brother Stan, who outlived the Cardinal, recounted a number of stories from their childhood. "He had a big head of blond hair, which he used to butt any opposition in any type of game. We used to taunt him at the dinner table and he would get very angry. After he received his First Holy communion, he asked the priest if he could serve Mass, even though it wasn't permitted to serve at the altar until fourth or fifth grade. 'You memorize the Latin, son, and I'll give it a thought,' the priest said, evidently thinking that a seven year old wouldn't be able to handle such a large task. His father tutored him and within a few months, young Jeff could recite the Latin phrases. He passed the exam with the parish priest and became a server, even though there were no cassocks or surplices to fit him."

Mary Jo found a religious sister at a convent for Nuns, one of whom had taught Jeff when he was a child. At 105 years, Sr. Ephrem was still alert and recalled Jeff, when he was in fourth grade. "Sure, I remember Jeffry very well,' she said and continued, "He had a permanent seat next to my desk, where naughty children had to sit. But he was a good kid with a sense of prayer. In fourth grade, he practiced football with the seventh and eighth graders. They let him play in the last game of the season and he butted a big kid from St. Lawrence's, and knocked the wind out of him. In sixth grade, he became a regular on the football team. That kid was competitive, I'll tell you that. His Dad was a cop on the Philadelphia Police Department and his mother, Maggie, would scold her children, when they didn't do well in their studies. When we had competition for spelling bees, he loved to win. He invited me to his first Mass in the Most Blessed Sacrament Church in Philly. Great kid all the way."

Mary Jo found that he loved his family very much. He was proud of his Dad, who was on the Philadelphia Police Force as a detective. He was wounded twice in the line of duty. His mother could trace her family tree back to Northern Ireland. "I'm off to Philadelphia in the morning" was a song that Martha "Maggie" O'Sullivan, his mother, had learned as a child. She had a quick wit. No one ever forget what she said of her husband when he was being buried, "I put his thirty eight in the coffin with him. Even the Beatific Vision wouldn't please him, if he wasn't packing." His grandfather had been chief of police and retired in good standing. Jeff loved to play sports with his brothers, and was close to them until his dying day. He would call his sister Marjory "Marge" almost every night. Her daughter also became a detective on the Philadelphia Police Force.

Jeff received three letters in sports, when he attended West Catholic in Philadelphia: for cross country, track and football, where he was an outstanding half back under the legendary coach, Danny Dougherty. In his senior year, he ran back three punts, two running from the wing, and caught four passes for touchdowns. He was offered scholarships from Dartmouth, William and Mary and Villanova. Jeff had other plans however. He wanted to be a priest, and chose a midwest diocese where his uncle (his mother's younger brother) was a priest and persuaded Jeff to come to his Diocese.

Mary Jo looked up classmates, who had gone through the seminary with Jeff. She found that he was respected by his classmates, played a lot of sports, and did extremely well in his studies. He did so well that the rector of the seminary advised the Bishop that Jeff would make an excellent candidate to send to the North American College in Rome. Jeff sailed on the ill-fated Andrea Doria, which later sank in a disastrous accident. He landed in Naples, where the rector of the college met Jeff and six other students from various dioceses throughout the United States. On their way to Rome on a bus, they stopped for lunch at the foot of Monte Casino. The waiter related how the blood had run down the steep hill from the Monastery, which was completely destroyed. The students begged the Rector to allow them to go up to the Monastery, which was then under reconstruction The students saw empty artillery shells, which were piled high around the area where the new Monastery was being built.

There were letters to his family from Rome, which had been preserved by his mother in brown boxes kept in the attic. Along with his letters, there were many snapshots of him and other students. There was a wealth of material in the letters which helped Mary Jo understand what life in Rome was like three years after the end of the Second World War. Jeff lived in the North American College and commuted by tram every day to the Jesuit Gregorian University. A fourth year student attending the "Greg" took Jeff aside and cautioned him about studies. "Never miss class," he said, "even if you don't like a professor or can't understand Latin, which is used in all the classes. Skipping class is the downfall of some talented seminarians. The student who doesn't study often fails, and is called back to his diocese. Go to the review classes provided in English here at the college. You'll do well." This advice proved to be very beneficial and certainly the key to be being successful in Rome. Jeff did his very best to carry out the senior student's advice. In four years, Jeff rarely missed the lectures of the outstanding Jesuit Professors, studied notes put together by senior students, and faithfully attended the review classes in English. Marks were given on a scale of five to ten. A five was a failure. In his first year, Jeff received mostly sevens (he stumbled along in Latin). The following year, he did fairly well and received an eight. One of the three Jesuit professors said in Italian, "bene, bene, bravo ragazzo" (you did well, son). In his third and fourth years, he fell short of tens, but received nines. In a coffee shop, Jeff met a German Jesuit, who had been his professor and examiner. The priest remembered him, and they struck up a friendship which lasted until the death of this outstanding scholar.

After attaining his Licentiate in theology, Jeff returned to his diocese and met with his Bishop. "We're proud of you, Jeff," the Bishop said, "all reports from your superiors in Rome are that you're dedicated to scholarship, good in Latin and have great perseverance. How would you like to go on for a Doctorate in Canon Law?" Jeff put his head down and avoided eye contact with the Bishop, who was known to be a no-nonsense fellow. Jeff was silent for a long time and tried to choose his words carefully. "Well, Your Excellency, with all due respect, I would prefer to study Dogma at Innsbruck where the Jesuits have a prestigious Theological School. I'm really not that interested in Canon Law. I would prefer to study Dogma with the Jesuits in Innsbruck." The Bishop's face became red and he just stared at Jeff with a piercing gaze. "Well, son," he said, "tell you what I'll do. I'll consider it, but don't get your hopes up." A week later, the Rector of the seminary and the Director of Studies came to his room in the seminary where he was staying. "They kind of leaned on me," as Jeff said later, "and persuaded me to take up Canon Law as they already had sufficient Theology Professors and the Diocese was in dire need of a Canon Lawyer." Out of obedience, Jeff followed the Bishop's orders. He returned to Rome, and after three years, received a Doctorate in Canon Law. For the defense of his dissertation, he received the first ten of his career. " Bene teipsum defendisti" (you defended yourself very well)), one examiner said as they drank coffee and cookies in a room in the University. Jeff was ready to return to the United States and begin priestly ministry.

After Jeff returned to his diocese, he was placed in parish ministry, which he enjoyed immensely. In later years, he related stories of his early days of pastoral care, and they were related throughout the diocese. He was put purposely with two "characters" in a row. The first pastor was a mega-manager (he thought), who smoked cigars and told yarns about the not so gifted priests in the diocese who were not so talented in the use of parish money, all the time giving the impression that he himself was an unrecognized genius. The second pastor was very parsimonious. He gave Jeff five bucks a week for spending money, and admonished him to call collect on any personal telephone calls. "In this outfit there are two kinds of pastors: savers and spenders. I always build a fund for serious repairs and the jackasses following me use it upon one stupid project after another. His nibs, Tommy (the Bishop), doesn't have a clue about the use of money. Tommy's a real winner, that guy. He gives the damndest permissions to those loonies."

After five years in parish work, Jeff was sent to the seminary to teach Canon Law. He became spiritual adviser to many students. After six years in the seminary, his next job was working on marriage cases in the Chancery Office. His background in Canon Law was put to good use. He was extremely helpful to the priests of the Diocese, in particularly complicated marriage cases. At a priest retreat, Jeff met the Bishop in the corridor who whispered to him, "keep up the good work, Jeff, we are watching you."

When the secretary to Bishop Hogan, Fr. John J. Carey, was made Auxiliary Bishop in Atlanta, Georgia, Jeff was selected to be secretary to the elderly Bishop. His duties entailed keeping the Bishop's schedule and dates in order. He also had to deal with official documents from the Pope and other leaders in the Church. Bishop Hogan was in ill health. Jeff often had a brandy with him in the evenings. He became the Bishop's confidant. He confided in Jeff, saying, "I pray every day for prudence in word and deed. I can offend people without even trying. When I say, 'Good Morning' to someone, the person wonders what I mean by that. I appreciate your loyalty, Jeff. The troops call you 'zipper lips' because you never give out information." Jeff found that Bishop Hogan, for all his outward gruffness, was like a marshmallow inside. Jeff worked for and with the Bishop for six years and carried the ball during Bishop Hogan's bout with cancer and continued after his death until a new Bishop was chosen by the Holy Father.

After the passing of Bishop Hogan, Bishop Carey was called back to succeed him. Naturally, he picked his own secretary. After a year in parish work, Jeff was informed that the Holy Father had chosen him to be Bishop of Memphis, Tennessee. He was well accepted there by the priests of the diocese, religious sisters and lay people, and after a period of adjustment, he became quite popular. He was criticized by some clerics for being "conservative." To that, Bishop Collins would retort, "Yeah, I conserve the traditions of the Church." The people were saddened, when he was designated to be Bishop of Houston Texas, where he stayed for a short stay of only five years. One day, he received a telephone call from the Apostolic Nuncio in Washington, telling him that he was being considered to be Archbishop of St. Louis. He was floored by this, and called the Cardinal in New York, a personal friend, and asked for his advice. "For the good of the Church, Jeff, accept," he counseled. Three months later, the Observatore Romano, the official newspaper of the Vatican, published the names of the new Archbishops, who would receive the Pectoral Cross affirming their call to a new responsibility in leading an Archdiocese. Archbishop Collins was sixty eight at the time. One year later Archbishop Collins was given the Red Hat as a symbol of complete dedication to the pastoral work of the Church, even if it entailed martyrdom. In a private meeting with the Polish Pope, the Holy Father jokingly said that Canon Lawyers were often chosen to be Bishops, but he added that that was in the past. "But I chose you myself, Jeffrey, because of your wisdom and prudence. Your Bishop and the professors of the seminary must have noticed your excellent qualities." Jeff finally realized what his Bishop had meant by the words, "We're watching you." At Blessed Sacrament parochial school and at West Catholic High School, his only desire was to be a priest and serve the people. In all these steps along the line, God was preparing him to take responsibility in the Church. In his last days, he reminisced that, even though he had many faults and had made some bad decisions, he knew without a doubt that the Blessed Mother was with him. He realized also, that through all the trouble and heart aches he had to encounter, in the end he was purified of his faults and spent his last days in prayer begging for God's mercy. He died after going to confession. He lay the whole night under the bench in the church and received the Sacred Anointment, just before he was taken to God.

Mary Jo Flanigan closed out her book with a sentimental story. When she was going through his effects in the attic of his old homestead, she found his mother's prayer book. When she opened it, she found a letter from Jeff when he was a first year theologian in Rome. It read: "Dear Mom and Dad, please pray for me that I'll be a good and faithful priest. I thank God for your love and understanding. I pray that my life will make you proud. Jeff" Mary Jo wrote that she thought Cardinal Collins was just that: a good and holy priest. Did Cardinal Collins need those extra and quiet hours to truly understand and appreciate the prayers of his parents from the time he left home to enter the seminary? Somehow he knew they had prayed for him, and that was all that mattered. In his solitude, he could begin to understand "The Makings of a Cardinal." That same solitude invited him to spend his last hours on earth with his rosary and to thank his devoted parents, whose prayers were the beginnings of his life as a priest, Bishop and Cardinal.

Fr. Father Nick's Last Drive

"I'm sorry, Father, but I'll have to take away your license for sixty days," Judge Mary Fallon said to Father Nicholas Laceto. After all, he had just been picked up for speeding by the State Police. In defense of himself, Fr. Nick said, "Well, Judge, I was on a legitimate sick call to an old man on a remote ranch out in the boonies." The judge countered that excuse saying "Yes, I've heard that tale from you in the past. You know or should know that we cannot condone speeding. You endanger yourself and worse, you endanger other people. Sheriff, take his license and escort him to his rectory." At the door, Father Nick turned to the Judge and said, "I saw your Dad at the barbeque, Mary. He's doing well after his heart attack. We missed you, though. I can remember when we had such a barbeque at your First Holy Communion." "Take care, Father," Judge Fallon said, "and stop speeding or I'll revoke your license all together. Then what would you do?"

The next day, Father Nick was taking a bus to a stop, where the migrant workers could pick him up. I could shoot over in half an hour, he thought. So now, it will take the whole day. Father Nick boarded the bus and took a seat in the front. As usual, he was sporting his roman collar in a white short- sleeved shirt for all to see. "Gregarious" could be called Father Nick's middle name, as he greeted each passenger who entered the bus. There was a woman who was visiting her son stationed in a nearby Air Force Base and a salesman from Houston. In addition, there was soldier in uniform and a black woman who said she had graduated from a catholic school. With undisguised sarcasm she added "my public school was separate and equal," and everyone laughed at this ridiculous meaning. Then two Latino youths boarded the bus and recognized Father Nick right away. "Where's your car, Padre?" they asked immediately. "We could see you coming with a trail of dust, whenever you visited the work sites. Boy, you seemed to be going a hundred miles an hour," one boy said in a voice that all could hear. "What? Me speed?" he answered. "Never, I stay around thirty or forty and just poke along" Nick answered with a chuckle. "Si, Si, Padre, I bet the police picked you up." All the people on the bus were following the dialog with interest. "Ah, the Judge took my license away for sixty days. I have to travel by bus until I come to a stop where the workers can pick me up. It's a pain in the neck," Nick answered. They all bantered together, as they went along the highway. He found out something about each passenger.

At the coffee break, the bus driver, a divorced Catholic but not an ex, told Nick that he was living with another woman who was also divorced. Then he asked, "Could I get it fixed up with the church, Padre? Because, you know, I really miss Holy Communion. What's that word 'annulment?' I hear if you got dough, they'll fix it up," he said. Fr. Nick explained, "Yeah, a lot of people, even in the Church think that, but it's not true. If you have a special reason, you can take it to a Diocesan Court and they will decide. Ask your Pastor. He'll be glad to help you out. I do the paper work for many Catholics. Some of them actually get an annulment. Even people, who in my judgment didn't have a chance, were granted an annulment." It takes a lot of time and piles of paper work, Nick thought, but that's part of a priest's job.

Father Nick used the bus to get around for sixty days. When that time was over, he retrieved his license from the Sheriff and vrooooom, he was off. Jimmy Conners, he thought to himself, thought that tennis was never a chore. Conners just loved tennis. And I love to drive!

Father Laceto (an abbreviated Czech name), who came from Texas soil, had worked his whole priestly life in rural Texas. It entailed constant driving, but that wasn't a burden he told his fellow priests. He learned early in life the first principles of driving. Once when he was a high school student, he failed to check the meter and ran out of gas on a remote highway. He waited hours under the blistering Texas sun before a State Trooper picked him up. If you ran out of gas on one of those highways, you could get robbed or even murdered. He remembered the old cowboy movies, when the star was walking through Death Valley with the "buzzards" up above and made it through by holding on to the tail of his "hose." The truckers and police all knew Fr. Nick. His code name with the truckers was "Ace." "Ace just went by, looks like he's on a sick call or something. Someday I'm going to pass HIM," the truckers would say. Everyone knew that he passed YOU, you did not pass HIM. The state police kind of looked the other way, when Nick would stay under ninety. Truckers coming the other way would flash their lights twice to signal to him that the cops were around the corner. Nick would slow down to about forty, and would wave to the police as he went by.

Nick had learned to drive on his father's farm, when he was about ten years old. He simply boarded his grandfather's car, figured out the gear system and drove around the farm. When he turned sixteen years old, he ventured out to the Texas State highways. He drove to high school and to sports events on Friday nights. Football was especially esteemed, and small towns often got "ringers" from other towns. The whole community would come to the games and cheer. Then, there were dances on Saturday nights.

Nick continued to serve Mass, even after he graduated from high school. In those rural areas it was difficult for primary school children to get to church and back and then go to school. Fr. Joe McCoyle, a Religious Order priest from Chicago, asked Nick outright if he had ever thought about becoming a priest. "Me?" answered Nick, "I think I would have trouble with Latin and those other subjects." "No," the priest answered, "all you need is average intelligence. Look at me. I got through. Think about it, son." Nick was surprised that they even asked him, but he was intrigued by the idea. He talked to his beloved grandparents who were immigrants from Eastern Europe. "Oh, Nicky, go for it," they said," You'll make a wonderful priest." So Nick talked to his parents who were equally supportive. He then decided to enter the diocesan seminary. He wanted to minister in his beloved Texas.

Fr. Nick did fairly well in his studies. He even passed Latin. On the football field, when he was quarterback, he would shout latin phrases, "Amo, amas, amat, hut." The quarterback on the other side would answer, "amamus, amatis, amant, hut." He did especially well in Philosophy. He loved to say the Latin Philosophy phrases, "Nemo dat quod non habet" (you can't give something you don't have) and, "Quid est hoc ad aeternitatem?" (What is this toward our eternal salvation?). When another seminarian put these same questions to him, he would reply, "Numquam audivi" (I never heard of it). When he returned from his vacation, his Latin Professor met him in the corridor and asked, "Bonum iter fecisti?" (Did you have a nice trip?). Nick didn't a have a clue what that meant and struggled with an answer " u-u-u-ti-que," (the Latin word for 'yes') he mumbled. The professor told the story in class which led to repeated ribbing from his classmates. "U-u-u-ti-que," they would repeat.

Eight years after entering the seminary Nick was ordained in his parish church. It was a big day for all the people of the town, many of whom were Catholics from Eastern Europe. There was a new young Bishop of the Diocese, whose roots went back to Mexico. He was cordial, humorous, and it seemed to Nick forward looking.

As a priest in rural Texas, Nick spent his life driving to remote ranchers, to hospitals, making sick calls, to old Folks' homes and with an outreach to the migrant workers from Mexico and Central America, who were working in Texas or were on their way to the enormous farms and orchards in California. The celebration of the Eucharist was often held in the open and in Spanish. The former Bishop had sent Nick to Mexico every summer during his four years of theology. Nick studied in a language school in Cuernavaca, one of the most beautiful cities in Mexico. During his time of study, he stayed with families. Thus, by the time he was ordained, he had a good grasp of the language. Nick's favorite places in Mexico were Monterey, Guadalajara, Mexico City and especially Cuernavaca. Nick grew to love the Latino culture: close family relationships, faith in God, and of course, Our Mother of

Guadalupe. They had a never-dying hope that their children would find a better life than theirs ("el norte," was always on their minds "to the north" or to United States).

Fr. Nick was welcomed by the migrant workers, who simply called him "padrecito" (affectionate word meaning "little father"). Nick visited the work and camp sites throughout his diocese and beyond. The workers knew Fr. Nick's phone number and would call each other before they asked if the priest could come to their site. Later, after cell phones were introduced, it was much easier to keep in contact. And the workers knew, when Fr. Nick was on the way. When they could see his car coming up the highway or through the back roads with the dust behind him, it was a signal, and the workers knew Fr. Nick was on the road.

One day, Nick received a call from the Chancery Office requesting him to meet with the Bishop at his convenience. The Bishop and Nick had been on rather familiar terms, ever since the Bishop had sent him to study in Mexico. The Bishop laid his cards right out on the table, saying, "the Dioceses in this area of Texas want to give better service to the migrant workers, and we are designating special priests to engage in this Apostolate. It entails a lot of driving, sometimes sleeping out under the stars and possible danger from robbers or the Farm Syndicate. I'd like you to think about this. I would never order you to take on such a burden. It would be completely your own decision." He put out his hand to shake Nick's, but Nick did not put out his. "A handshake later, after you hear what I have to say," Nick answered in a serious tone. "I don't have to think about it. I'll do it with your blessing. This is what you trained me for. I don't mind driving. It's not a burden, it's a pleasure. I'm not afraid of anything. I'll do it." The Bishop stared at this good, young Priest for a long time. Then he put his hand out again. They shook hands and then embraced.

Thus, Father Nick began a whole new apostolate to migrant workers. The only condition that the Bishop put on his work was that, as far as possible, he would have to stay in parishes within driving distance of the camps and work sites. The Bishop sent out a pastoral letter to all the pastors, in which he explained Nick's work and asked for hospitality. The response of the pastors was overwhelming, and Nick was received graciously wherever he went. He could shower, have a good meal, could rest with confidence and best of all, could enjoy priestly fraternity. He never failed to present the pastor with a bottle of California wine. "My workers harvest those grapes," he would say. The pastors were amazed at the amount of driving Nick had to do. "It's no problem with me. I've been driving, since I was ten years old on my Dad's farm," Nick would answer.

Nick didn't consider it part of his mandate to get involved in labor disputes between the farmers and the migrant workers. However, he did not step aside, when he saw outrageous injustice. He would speak quietly but firmly to the leaders of the farm syndicate. "Hey, these are good family people, who only want a fair shake. I don't want any trouble and I would not go to the Media, but I ask you for a solution to their requests. More often than not, amicable solutions were found to the disputes. The workers were delighted, when they got a new outhouse, a truck, or tools. Father Nick became respected on both sides of the aisle. And so the years passed. New workers, men and women, legal and illegal, continued to come looking for work.

When the migrant workers heard that Padrecito was going to celebrate his fiftieth anniversary of ordination to the Priesthood, a network of phone calls went out through Texas and California. The workers were going to celebrate in a big Latino way. They hired a park, set up tables, and put a special table out under a big tree for the celebration of the Mass outdoors. There were fifty guitars at the Mass, which was very emotional. The retired old Bishop, now in his nineties, who had trained Nick, gave the homily in Spanish in which he praised Nick's zeal, his good humor, and his driving (which caused loud laughs). He also praised the workers for their dedication to their families and complete trust in Our Lady. After the Mass, there were speeches (with references to Speedy Gonzales), toasts, songs, dancing and feasting. When the shadows grew long across the field, a leader took the mike and said, "Silence, please. It's beginning to get dark and we have long drives home this evening, but we have come to the main part of our celebration. Okay, boys, bring it in." From the other side of the grounds, a brand new Honda was driven across the field and stopped in front of the place where Nick and the Bishop were seated. There was cheering, applause and the distinctive Latino whistling. Father Nick could not believe that this new automobile was for him. He was handed holy water, and he walked around the car sprinkling it with one hand and blessing it with the other. He then kissed the fender and boarded the car. He drove all around the park, waving to all his Latino friends. Then, he stopped before the old Bishop and asked him to get in. They drove around again, this time with the Bishop blessing all present. Nick knew that he couldn't drive the new Honda home before it was registered (he knew someone would bring it up by truck). The Bishop took the mike and again thanked everyone for their loyalty and kindness to his priest, Father Nick. Nick had the last word. He broke down a few times and thanked the people for their love and affection. Then he drove the Bishop home in his old car. When they were going over eighty, the Bishop tightened his seat belt, put his feet firmly on the floor boards and grasped the dashboard with his hands. There were white knuckles that you have never seen before! Nick, seeing that his old friend was terrified, slowed down to sixty. A trucker passed them and immediately noted on his wireless, "Ace is out and travelling with another person. This is the time to pass him. You'll never get another chance." The truckers struggled to pass Nick on the highway and gave a loud horn as they passed. "You seem to know all the truckers," the Bishop said. "Yeah," answered Nick, "they love to pass me."

The standing Bishop, who had heard all about Nick's apostolate, granted him a sabbatical to do what he wanted. Nick wouldn't dare take his new car to Mexico. So he drove down in his old Chrysler. It was a perfect vacation. He drove to all the places he had visited, when he was a student, and since the workers in Texas and California told their families that Father Nick was coming, everywhere he went he met relatives of his friends in America. "We heard all about you, Padrecito," they said. "We hear you drive very fast." He answered, "Well, that's me, I guess. I've been driving since I was ten years old."

It was only a few months after his sabbatical ended that Father Nick Laceto was found dead in his car on the shoulder of the road. A trucker called the State Police and informed them that there seemed to a problem off the highway. He guessed it was "Ace". He then wired his buddies that "Ace" was slumped over the wheel of his car and was either dead or unconscious. It was Nick in a new white shirt with his roman collar. An autopsy revealed that Nick had died of a massive stroke. Fortunately, he was able to steer the car off the road before he died.

The funeral Mass was held in the Cathedral. The Bishop of the Diocese celebrated the Mass and Nick's old friend, the Bishop who had prepared him for work with migrant workers, gave an emotional homily. Many guitars played at the Spanish Mass. There was a lot of weeping and a eulogy by one of the leaders of the workers, who spoke of "Speedy Gonzales." "We could see his car coming in the distance with a lot of dust in the wake."

The migrant workers lined up on either side of the street as the hearse carrying Father Nick drove off. They waved handkerchiefs and shouted "Padrecito. Padrecito." Then they jumped into their cars to follow the hearse to the cemetery. On prime time the local TV station showed a clip featuring the hearse moving slowly among the Latino people. The viewers were amazed at this touching scene. It was Father Nick Laceto's last drive.

Father Henry's New Dimension

The following is a chapter from the book "Our Journey to Rome" by Noah Marksman.

The first time we met Fr. Henry Powers was when he was seen playing kick ball with our daughter, Joanie, who had Down Syndrome. Joan was in her mid-twenties, but looked much younger. We were not blessed with other children, so Joanie was the love of our lives. Janice, my wife, looked out the window and saw Joanie playing kick ball with an elderly gentleman, who was wearing black trousers and a grey sweat shirt. So Janice went out on the deck and introduced herself, "Hi, I'm Janice Marksman. Thank you for playing kick ball with our daughter." "Glad to meet you, Ma'am," the priest answered. "I'm Henry Powers, the new priest in residence here. I retired from teaching and this is my very first parish. I just moved in yesterday and saw that the yard was a mess. As I was doing some raking, Joanie here asked me to play kick ball. I said 'sure.' I hope you don't mind. By the way, you wouldn't be the Janice Marksman the famous poet, would you?" "Yep, that's me. The emphasis definitely is not on 'famous.' I'm delighted some one reads my stuff." "Well," continued Fr. Henry, "I really like your work and you have received many awards." Janice made a deep bow and said, "Well, I'm overwhelmed." "By the way," Henry went on, "Noah Marksman wouldn't be your husband, would he? I was giving a lecture at Shane College and I remember I met him." "Yep, you got that right, too," Janice answered. "Well he too is one of my favorites. His writing on the First World War is both provocative and riveting reading." "He will be delighted to hear that, Reverend. He should be home soon. You'll have to come over for coffee some time," Janice said and gave an open invitation. "Imagine that," the priest answered, "meeting two of my favorite writers and they live just next door." Joanie, who was hoping to play more kick ball, got bored with the conversation, picked up her soccer ball and said, "See ya tomorrow, Henry." She went directly into the house. All this, Janice explained to me when I arrived home in the evening from Shane College.

Joanie and Janice told me about the new minister, who had just moved in next door. Joanie invited him to play kick ball, and he joined right in. I admonished Joanie that it was not good manners to invite an elderly man to play kick ball like that. Joanie only answered, 'Oh, Henry don't mind. He said I could call him any time.'" Janice related how she had talked to the Reverend from the deck. "He seemed very cultured and urbane," she said, "He is quite elderly to be starting off as a parish priest. He has read my poetry and your work on history. I gather he is some kind of a scholar himself." It did not take long to find Henry Powers on the internet. "Listen to these credentials," I said to Janice. "He has a Master's degree in Greek and Latin from Catholic University in Washington, a Licentiate in Theology from the Gregorian University in Rome and a Doctorate in Biblical Studies from the Biblicum in Rome. He has written twenty books and published many articles in prestigious magazines. He taught summer school at Shane College a few years ago, and evidently he remembers me from that time. He seems to be an outstanding scholar." "And a perfect gentleman," added Janice. "Just think, he is a minister, a scholar and an elderly man who did not find it beneath him to play soccer kick ball with a child. He must be some kind of guy. We'll have to get to know him." "Henry's my friend. He likes to play kick ball," Joanie said.

So as it turned out, the Reverend played kick ball with Joanie frequently, and they got acquainted. Joanie called him Henry from the beginning, but we continued to call him Reverend. Somewhere back in our training, we had learned the verse from Scripture, "Let none among you be called Father." Even though Janice and I had never been baptized into any sect, our families embraced churches according to the type of Pastor there was. Although we were from different back grounds, we had given up on religion altogether. We joined the secular society in the academic world and were perfectly content. However, the stories of Maria Monk and others that we heard when we were young left an indelible impression. In our subconscious, we were anti-Catholic and didn't know it. The academic world we lived in enforced this mentality. Henry said, "Just call me Henry. Heck, we're next door neighbors. I never dreamed two of my favorite writers would end up living near me." "And we," answered Janice, "never dreamed that an eminent Scripture scholar would play kick ball with our daughter." It was the beginning of a lasting friendship.

One evening, Joanie called from the television room that Henry was on television. We raced to the room and found that Reverend Powers was a member of a panel discussion on World Religions. There were two Jewish Rabbis, a Hindu woman in a sari, two Islam Imans, a Protestant minister from Harvard and Henry representing the Catholic Church. It was a very civil discussion on tolerance. Henry in a laidback way spoke humbly about his Church's history and pointed out that the Pope had spoken out publicly to ask forgiveness for the lack of tolerance in the past. We thought that Henry gave an excellent impression for his Church. In this professional atmosphere, Henry didn't appear that he was the type of person who would play kick ball with a child. We found out too from other sources that, besides being a scholar, he was also a humanist. He was excellent on the piano and often played at concerts. Evidently, he could have been a professional musician. We also learned that his grandparents on both sides were coal miners from upstate Pennsylvania.

One Sunday after the Mass as the Reverend was greeting the parishioners as they exited the church, he noticed Joanie beside him also shaking hands with the people. "Hi, I'm Joanie. Henry is my friend. We play kick ball together." After that, little by little, Joanie became known throughout the parish.

One Sunday, Joanie attended Mass and attempted to receive Communion along with the other believers. However, the Reverend refused her and sent her back to her bench. Joanie was deeply offended and stormed out of the church. "Henry's mean. Henry's mean," she said. From what we gathered, she had put out her hand to receive the white bread but was not permitted to do so by the priest. That afternoon the Reverend appeared and apologized for the affair. We explained to Joanie that the bread was reserved only for those who were baptized, and therefore she was not permitted. But Joanie was still pouting until the Reverend asked her to play kick ball and then all was forgiven.

Joan continued to attend Mass after that, but she never went up to receive Communion. But without fail, she greeted people after the service. Janice and I had private conversations about allowing Joanie to get baptized, so that she could receive Communion along with the other believers. We had some serious reservations about this big step for our family, since both Janice and I, even though we believed in the existence of some higher power, we did not participate in any Christian denomination. My parents really had no definite religion, even though we had a Bible in our home that covered about five generations. Janice remembered that her grandmother was a Catholic but had stopped practicing after she married grandpa who was a nonpracticing Mormon. Janice's parents had floundered between one denomination and another. Janice herself had never received any training in the teachings of the Bible. We both had one thing in common and that was a deep seated antipathy toward Roman Catholics, whom we considered to be a group of immigrants who lived in a ghetto and did not send their children to public schools. They also, we heard, held allegiance to a foreign power. Above that, we had a Maria Monk mentality about priests and nuns. Somewhere along the way, we had picked up this quaint American tradition of anti-Catholicism. This idea was emphasized even more in the academic world. So, allowing our daughter to join such a denomination was almost unthinkable. The only things that swung us in that direction were Joanie's desire for Communion and the apparent goodness of the Reverend who was, if nothing else, a perfect gentleman. We therefore agreed to ask the Reverend, if he might allow Joanie to enter the Catholic Church. Henry was very happy to hear of this request. "Sure," he said, "the only things I need are your permission and Joanie's agreement. You would have to promise to allow Joanie to go to Mass and help her persevere in her decision." Henry said that it would not be appropriate to teach Joanie catechism in the Rectory. He recommended that he teach her right in our kitchen.

The Reverend came over once a week for over a year, and instructed Joanie with the help of a highly illustrated Bible for children and an introduction to First Communion book for first grade students. He had Joanie memorize some key phrases from the Bible: I am the Bread of life, I am the good Shepherd, Love is kind, This is my body, This is My blood. Joanie repeated these phrases over and over again. Henry also taught her the hymn On Angels Wings. It was at this period of her catechesis that Joanie began to sit in the first bench directly in front of the Lectionary Stand. Henry announced to the congregation that Joanie was a "catechumen", which meant she was preparing for Baptism. Everyone applauded and welcomed Joanie into the community.

When the time for Baptism approached, Father (we had finally gotten over that hurdle) told us that we would need a sponsor. That is, someone to be Joanie's God Mother. We racked our brains trying to think of someone in good standing in the Roman persuasion. Then Janice remembered that her publisher, Carol Lufts, was a fervent Catholic. Carol, who had personally edited Janice's books, was delighted to be Joanie's sponsor. Joanie had met this publisher before and called her Aunt Carol. Carol's company had also published one of Father Henry's books, so they were already acquainted.

Joanie was baptized the following Easter at the long Holy Saturday ceremony. Joanie and Carol brought up the Bread and Wine at the Offertory. Joanie took for her Baptismal name, Joan of Arc, the famous French saint. She also received Confirmation and her First Holy Communion on the same night. Father held a special party for Joanie in the parish hall. Of course, Joanie gave a speech which she had prepared well, "Thank you, Henry. I love you. Thank you, Mommy and Daddy. I love you. Thank you, Aunt Carol. I love you. And everybody, thank you. I love you." There was long applause and not a few tears

Joanie died a year later from complications arising from pneumonia. She was anointed by Father Henry with Sacred Oil. She died in her sleep right before our eyes. It was the saddest day of our lives.

At the Funeral Mass, Father Henry related how he and Joanie had met. "I was raking leaves in the back yard of our church when Joanie came up and said, 'Hey, mister, wanna play kick ball with me?' She was innocence itself, guileless, and full of humor. She was close to God. The Heavenly Father sent her to me to teach me that faith is not only in the head but also in the heart. With all my academic achievements, I had not learned that dimension of faith. Joanie taught it to me. We played kick ball together almost every day. When she got tired, she would pick up the soccer ball and say, 'See ya tomorrow, Henry.' Thank you, Lord, for sending

Joanie to me. Janice and Noah are so wonderful in allowing Joanie to be born. She was never a hardship to them. She brought them joy and happiness."

Janice and I were received into the Catholic Church a few years after Joanie's death. It was not an easy step for me, but for Janice it was an uncomplicated decision. She waited for me. "I won't take the step without you," she said. The priest who succeeded Father Henry taught me the meaning of the Bible, the Sacraments, the Ten Commandments and the Catholic Liturgy. At one point, he told me I was carrying a lot of "baggage," which was very true. In my youth and in my academic career, I had absorbed many false teachings about the Church. Little by little I was won over. In the end though, there were two factors which aided me in my decision: one was the memory of my beloved daughter singing On Angels' Wings, and the other was a kind and humble priest, who did not think it was beneath him to play with a child. I took the name Henry for my Baptismal Name and Janet decided on Joan of Arc. We don't use these names officially in society, but we treasure our Christian names to remind us that we are children of God. And our greatest joy is receiving the Bread of Life.

Noah Marksman

Fr. Thomas P. Dwyer, Retired Villanova, June 2010

Profile of the Author

Fr. Thomas P. Dwyer of the Augustinian Order (founder of Villanova University) was born in Bryn Mawr on October 23, 1932. The family moved to Ardmore when Thomas was an infant. Although the Dwyers were much closer to St. Colmans Church in Ardmore, they attended St. Denis in Havertown (their home parish). Fr. Dwyer attended St. Denis parochial school. The school was run by the Mercy Sisters from Merion, Pennsylvania.

From St. Denis, our author proceeded to West Catholic High School for three years before entering Augustinian Academy in Staten Island. He graduated from there in 1950. After a year in the Novitiate, he went to Villanova University and graduated in 1955 with a B.A. in Philosophy. In the fall of the same year, Fr. Dwyer was sent to the Augustinian International School in Rome. He was ordained to the priesthood in 1958 and returned to America in July, 1959. He immediately volunteered to be a missionary in Japan where he ministered in Tokyo, Nagoya, Fukuoka and Nagasaki.

Fr. Dwyer, because of illness, retired to the Augustinian Monestary at Villanova in 2010. He lives a peaceful and happy life there. Fr. Dwyer recently published the memoirs of his ministry in Japan. Once can find the book on Amazon under the title "Memoirs of My Missionary Life in Japan 1959 to 2010."

CPSIA information can be obtained at www.ICGtesting.com
Printed in the USA
BVOW09s1112250714

360433BV00003B/40/P